Walter Ego v6.03

A modern comedy

By

Andrew Crossland

Characters

WALTER EMERSON (25-49) – Walter is a cocky, confident, man. He was diagnosed with a number of illnesses at a young age. He doesn't take his condition seriously and often makes jokes about it. He sold a computer business he started at college making him very wealthy. He has lived life, from the age of nineteen to the present day, in luxury. He made sure he lived every day to the fullest, knowing he was likely to die young. His symptoms are now getting worse. One of his illnesses affects his memory which is the ailment that upsets him the most.

DR. GOWER (30-75) – Walter's private doctor. He takes his job, as well as Walter's treatment, very seriously. He doesn't respond well to Walter's jokes and sense of humour at first, but the more time he spends with him, the more he begins to loosen up. He is a 'true' friend, caring only for Walter's well-being and not his fortune.

JANICE HOPSON (25-49) – Janice is the same age as Walter and was his college girlfriend. They broke up as she felt his work was more important than her. They have kept minimal contact since then, still caring a lot for him, as a friend, only. She still finds him amusing and genuinely wants to help him.

DEREK JAMES (20-69) – Janice's new boyfriend of nearly two years. He doesn't like the relationship between her and Walter and attempts to belittle him whenever he can. He has his own sense of humour and uses this in his constant childish battles with Walter.

FRAN PHILLIPS (18-45) – Fran is an upper-class girl that Walter meets on the internet. She talks very posh and has old fashioned manners. She doesn't respond well to common banter. Her only more 'modern' trait is her excessive use of her mobile phone.

ZARA COOPER (18-45) – Zara is the other girl that Walter meets on the internet. She is a more modern girl whose type is the 'bad boy'. She's down to earth and knows exactly what she wants. She is very confident.

OLIVIA (Any) – A brummy with foul mouth and a knack for cleaning. Everything must be clean, and she is oblivious to most other things that go on around her.

Contents

Props List

Tea cup
Various plates of dinner food with at least 1 steak
Bowl of tomato soup
Cutlery
Dinner trays
Monet painting
Long-haired wig
Motorbike helmet
Upright vacuum with removable chamber
Laptop
Television remote
White throw
Dishcloth
Mop & Bucket
Mobile Phone
Coat stand
Framed photo of dog and Walter
Framed photo of Walter and Steve McQueen
Pen and clipboard with medical notes
Floor plant
Cardboard box
Framed certificates
Trophies
Coin collection
Various antiques, such as weapons and vases
Urn filled with ashes
Hospital bed
Drip stand
ECG monitor
Zara profile page
Wine bottles and glasses
Olivia's cleaning list
Gardening gloves

Act 1 Scene 1 - Opening

*The set is two rooms of a mansion. SR is the dining room containing a small, but elaborate, dining table accompanied by two chairs. There is a free-standing coat rack by the SR exit as well as a shelf on the upstage wall with numerous awards and certificates, a coin collection, some ancient vases and some antique weapons. The other side of the stage, which is separated by a low rising divide to give the impression of an interior wall, is the living room. There is a cupboard door at the back of this room as well as a potted plant. A sofa, with a large white throw over the back, is facing the audience which is where the TV would hang on the "fourth wall." There is a small semi-circle shaped shelf on the back wall upon which an urn sits. In the middle of this room, currently blocking the sofa and pointed at the "television", is a hospital bed. By the bed is a drip stand and an E.C.G. monitor. A closed laptop is leant against the side of the soda. There is no side wall at either side of the stage to give the impression that the rooms are much larger. There are two doorways on the upstage wall, one in each room, which leads to a small corridor and is used for access between the two. Exiting SR leads to the front door, hallway and the toilet. SL exit leads to the kitchen and the rest of the mansion. The lights come up on just the living room. **DR. GOWER** stands by the bed looking at a chart. **WALTER** lays in the bed hooked up to the machines.*

DR. GOWER It's not good news, I'm afraid. Your condition is worsening far more rapidly than I'd originally thought. You have deteriorated immensely since last week.

WALTER *(care-free)* I still get a lollipop for being a good boy, though, don't I, Doc?

DR. GOWER Did you even hear what I just said?

WALTER I've told you before. I've made my peace with dying. As long as I don't lose my mind first, that is.

DR. GOWER That should be the least of your worries. You'll most likely be dead before you notice any obvious symptoms of memory loss.

WALTER And said so staid. I'm not used to hearing the 'd' word from you. You normally dance around the subject.

DR. GOWER Yes, well, seeing you always make light of the matter must be rubbing off on me.

WALTER *(jumping up out of the bed and removing his attachments)* I do that, because I feel fine.

DR. GOWER But you're <u>not</u> fine.

WALTER As long as I die before I lose my memory, I'll be happy.

DR. GOWER There is a chance that, over the coming weeks, your memory could get steadily worse. Nothing too drastic. Probably just the odd episode here and there.

WALTER I think I can handle that.

DR. GOWER How are you feeling in yourself? I've seen it plenty of times. Patients, much like yourself who have little time left, struggle, understandably, with some serious mental health issues towards the end. It's best that you don't keep things bottled up. You can talk to me about that stuff too if need be.

WALTER You don't have to be so nice, Doc. Don't worry, I'll make sure that you're in the will.

DR. GOWER You know that's not why I'm asking. Your health is my number one concern. And besides, my salary as your private physician isn't bad, you know.

WALTER I <u>do</u> know. I sign the cheques.

DR. GOWER Just try and be serious with me, for once.

WALTER *(sighs)* Well, I did ring my ex-girlfriend from college the other day. That's probably a good indicator that my mental health isn't at its best, right?

DR. GOWER Any reason, or…

WALTER I wanted to see what she was up to these days.

DR. GOWER Are you having regrets of some sort?

WALTER Not regrets, as such. Just trying to catch up with an old friend before I croak it. And, to be truthful, I was hoping for a bit of fun before I passed.

DR. GOWER 'A bit of fun?'

WALTER Yeah. You know. *(thrusting his hips)* A bit of fun!

DR. GOWER *(rolls his eyes)* So why this girl? Why not one of the hundred others?

WALTER Janice was the most serious relationship I've ever had. She was truly special.

DR. GOWER Then why aren't you still with her?

WALTER <u>She</u> ended things. Said I cared more about my work than her. I can see why she would think that. It consumed me at the time. I can't really blame her for leaving me.

DR. GOWER I bet she was kicking herself afterwards when you sold your business. She could have been a millionaire too, if she'd stayed with you.

WALTER I doubt she was bothered. She's not very materialistic. She'd have been happy in poverty as long as we had each other. Maybe I should have felt the same. My wealth seems a bit meaningless now.

DR. GOWER It's not uncommon for people, like yourself, with cruelly short life expectancies, to focus on the more 'important' things towards the end. Would you do things differently if you had that time again?

WALTER I'm not sure, Doctor. I may only be living a third of the life of a normal man, but I have lived the life of <u>three</u> men. Most people won't get to experience <u>half</u> the things <u>I've</u> done in their whole lifetime. The way I see it, the universe is just balancing itself out.

DR. GOWER Not even for this ex-girlfriend you mention? Would you not change things so that you could have spent <u>that</u> time with her?

WALTER *(returning to his usual self)* No need to get so serious, Doc. Like I said; I've lived my life. I just want a bit more fun with the ladies, if you know what I mean.

DR. GOWER If that was the case, then you could have rung any one of your many conquests, but you chose this particular girl.

WALTER The reason I rang <u>her</u>, was because I also need someone to leave everything to.

DR. GOWER What about family?

WALTER I don't have any.

DR. GOWER None at all?

WALTER Nope. My dad went the same way I'm going. My mother killed herself. No grandparents, no kids, no siblings, no nothing.

DR. GOWER Are you this blasé with all the negative aspects of your life?

WALTER Yes. I think it helps onlookers to have less sympathy for me. Does it?

DR. GOWER *(pondering)* Yes, I suppose it does. Well, what about friends?

WALTER Oh I have plenty of those, but believe me, they don't need my money. That's quite bad isn't it? That all my friends are rich. As my life changed, so did my friends.

DR. GOWER I couldn't comment. I'm not from <u>that</u> world. So this... Janice... How did she respond to your phone call?

WALTER Not well. She hung up.

DR. GOWER Did you tell her you were ill?

WALTER No. We spoke for a bit, and then I basically asked if she wanted to get back on it.

DR. GOWER 'Get back on it?'

WALTER You know. *(giving a thrust of the hips)* Get back on it!

DR. GOWER Charming! I'm guessing it's at that point she hung up?

WALTER It was a little embarrassing. I'll be happy if I never see her again.

The doorbell rings.

WALTER Someone at the door, Doc.

DR. GOWER And?

WALTER Are you going to answer it?

DR. GOWER If you wanted someone to answer the door, you should have hired a butler.

WALTER You're always complaining about the last staff member that I hired.

DR. GOWER The cleaner? Her language is atrocious. 'F' this and 'f' that.

WALTER I know, but it's the way she words things. She cracks me up.

DR. GOWER It's beside the point; I will not be taking up butler duties.

WALTER Fine. I'll go answer the door... *(faking, over dramatic)* Oh... oooh... urgh. Oh, Doctor. It hurts! The pain! I need to lie down. *(climbs into the bed)* I think it would be detrimental to my health to answer the door. As my doctor, you need to see that my best interests are met.

WALTER has a cheeky grin on his face. DR. GOWER gives a sigh and starts to head out of the room.

WALTER Wait!

DR. GOWER What?

WALTER Doctor, doctor. I've got a strawberry stuck in my ear.

DR. GOWER Don't worry, I've got a cream for that.

WALTER Dammit!

DR. GOWER I've told you, I've heard them all before. You're not going to find one that I haven't.

WALTER I will, don't you worry.

The doorbell rings again. WALTER gives DR. GOWER an indicating nod towards the door. He leaves the living room via the arched doorway and heads into the dining room. The lights come up in there and go down in the living room. He exits SR to answer the front door, returning shortly after followed by JANICE and DEREK.

JANICE Sorry about our dirty shoes. The path to the house is really muddy.

DR. GOWER *(mimicking a butler)* Pay it no heed. And who should I tell Mr. Emerson is calling?

JANICE Janice. Janice Hopson.

DR. GOWER Janice, you say? *(smirks)* Interesting.

OLIVIA enters from the hallway SR.

OLIVIA Oh fucking hell. Who's gone and got muddy footprints all over the lobby carpet? It's fucking slarted.

DR. GOWER Forget that for now, Olivia. Let me introduce you to...

OLIVIA *(cutting in)* Oh no I can't leave it like that can I? I'll just give it the once over with the vac.

OLIVIA grabs a vacuum cleaner from off stage right and turns it on. She is pushing it around the area just off SR as well as where JANICE and DEREK have just come in. She is banging into their heels and they, as well as DR. GOWER, have to dodge out of her way. DR. GOWER is shouting at her, but is drowned out by the sound of the vacuum cleaner. She turns it off so that the last of DR. GOWER's speech is heard.

DR. GOWER *(shouting)* ...shove it where the sun doesn't shine!

OLIVIA There, that's much better, ain't it? A bit of cleaning does the place wonders.

DR. GOWER *(to JANICE)* I shall tell Walter that you've arrived.

DEREK *(sarcastically)* Thanks, Jeeves.

DR. GOWER gives DEREK a stern look. JANICE hits DEREK on the arm.

DR. GOWER Olivia, please don't embarrass us in front of our guests.

OLIVIA Oi, ya cheeky fuck. I'm a delight to be around.

DR. GOWER huffs and heads through the arched doorway.

OLIVIA *(to JANICE)* Hello. I'm Olivia. The cleaner.

DEREK This guy has his own cleaner?

OLIVIA *(looking at DEREK'S shoes)* Your shoes are a bit worn down, mister. They're all tarnished. They want chucking in the bin.

DEREK *(walking away from her)* We're not all made of money.

OLIVIA There's your problem. You're a bit heavy on your feet. You must be like an elephant. If you carry on, I'll have to put you in a pair of wooden clogs. I'll take them to the cobblers in the morning if you want?

DEREK I'll pass, thanks.

OLIVIA *(to herself)* Well, you can't educate pork. *(exits SR taking the vacuum cleaner with her)*

DEREK *(looking around the room)* I can't believe that I'm here.

JANICE I told you to stay at home.

DEREK Are you kidding? Your ex-boyfriend rings you up, and two days later you want to visit? No chance was I letting you come here on your own.

JANICE I told you, I'm worried about him. The way he was talking. Something's wrong with him. He didn't have to say it. I just knew.

DEREK *(sarcastically)* Oh great. So now you're like kindred spirits or something?

JANICE rolls her eyes. DEREK wanders around the dining room looking at various things.

DEREK He must be worth a bob or two, this bloke.

JANICE You could say that. He wasn't rich when I went out with him, but I've followed his success in the newspapers.

DEREK What was he in the papers for?

JANICE He's done a few notable things.

DEREK *(picking up a couple of framed awards and reading them)* One hundred and ninety seventh on the rich list! Humanitarian of the year!

JANICE He did always say he would give a lot to charity if he ever made it big.

DEREK I'll say he made it very big! Why did you ever leave this guy?

JANICE Money isn't everything, Derek.

DEREK I know, but there's money and then there's money!

The lights flip over lighting up the living room and leaving the dining room in darkness.

DR. GOWER *(mimicking a butler's voice)* A Janice Hopson to see you, sir.

WALTER *(laughing)* That was very good that. You sounded just like a real butler… Whaaaaaaa?

DR. GOWER Janice... Isn't she the...

WALTER Yep.

DR. GOWER Your first love...

WALTER Yep.

DR. GOWER The one you said you'd be happy if you never saw again.

WALTER That's the one.

DR. GOWER *(smirking)* Well, this should be fun.

WALTER *(getting excited)* Maybe she's had a change of heart. Maybe she wants a piece.

DR. GOWER 'A piece'?

WALTER Yeah, you know. *(jumping out of bed and thrusting his hips again)* A piece!

DR. GOWER Made a full recovery then, I see.

WALTER Yes, I feel loads better. And <u>you</u> made an excellent butler. Maybe you <u>should</u> take on the role alongside your medical duties. I'll pay of course.

DR. GOWER I don't think so. Doctor, remember... not slave.

WALTER Exactly! <u>Doctor</u>! And it's for the sake of my <u>health</u> that you do any thing I ask to make sure that I don't overexert myself. Especially if I'm going to be getting some extra action over the next few weeks.

DR. GOWER 'Extra action'?

WALTER YES! *(frustrated now that he has to explain again)* Extra action! *(thrusts hips more vigorously this time)*

DR. GOWER sighs and looks away.

WALTER What's the matter, Doc? Don't you like it when I talk about sex?

DR. GOWER I just don't think it's necessary to be the topic of every one of our conversations of late.

WALTER *(rolling his eyes)* Not <u>every</u> conversation.

DR. GOWER I just think that some subjects should be handled more delicately.

WALTER Delicately? Didn't you ever go to college?

DR. GOWER Of course I did. But I took my studies very seriously. I didn't have time for fun and games.

WALTER So you never joked around with friends?

DR. GOWER Not excessively.

WALTER You never had girls around for a bit of cheeky?

DR. GOWER 'A bit of cheeky'?

WALTER Yes!

*WALTER races towards **DR. GOWER** bends him over the bed in a compromising position. **WALTER** is thrusting him from behind, simulating sex.*

WALTER A bit of cheeky!

DR. GOWER is mortified and is shouting at him to stop.

JANICE *(entering this side of the stage)* Excuse me? We've been waiting a long time and we... *(spotting the two of them)* Walter?

*WALTER and **DR. GOWER** freeze in their position and stare at JANICE. All three have shocked looks on their faces. This scene is held for a moment until **DEREK** also enters this side of the stage.*

DEREK I'm not waiting in there on my own and... Oh... I see... It's one of those kind of parties. *(to **JANICE**)* I see why things didn't work out between you two.
DR. GOWER No, no, it's not like that. I was just...
WALTER Come on, Doc. Don't be shy. We're all adults here. *(giving him a slap on the bottom leaving him gob-smacked)* Hello, Janice, lovely to see you. *(giving her a kiss on the cheek)* You look as beautiful as ever. *(turning to **DEREK**)* Hello. I don't think we've met. Walter Emerson. Nice to meet you. *(taking his hand for a shake)*
DEREK Derek James.
WALTER Are you Janice's friend?
DEREK Her boyfriend!

WALTER's face drops and he drops DEREK's hand. DR. GOWER laughs. WALTER turns and gives him a serious look. He stops laughing.

DR. GOWER I'll make myself scarce. *(exits SL)*
WALTER *(to **JANICE**)* So you're not here for a quick scuttle then?
DEREK 'A quick scuttle?'
WALTER Yes. *(thrusting his hips)* A quick scuttle. *(to the heavens)* Does no one speak my language?
JANICE No I didn't. I came to see if you were all right. Judging by the hospital bed, my suspicions were right. Something's wrong with you.

WALTER *(wheeling the bed off SL)* Nothing to worry about. Just a routine check-up. Doctor Gower is one of the best in the country.

JANICE Don't give me that. I could tell that there was something wrong when you rang me. Why don't you just tell me what it is?

WALTER You were always so cute when you got serious.

DEREK *(squaring up to **WALTER**)* Ok, pal. Just because you're some rich, generous, do-gooder... I have no problem fighting you.

WALTER Oh, you've seen my awards? Did you see the one for national boxing champion?

DEREK *(backing down)* National wha...?

WALTER *(inflating his chest)* That's right!

JANICE Knock it off, Walter. Tell me what's wrong. Why did you <u>really</u> ring me?

WALTER You won't like it.

JANICE Just tell me.

WALTER I was hoping to re-kindle our romance. So, what do you say? Why not ditch Dexter and come back to a <u>real</u> man?

DEREK It's Derek!

WALTER Whatever.

JANICE Grow up, Walter. If that really is your reason, why now? Why after all this time.

WALTER If you really want to know the truth, I'll tell you. *(genuinely)* I'm dying.

JANICE What?

DEREK Oh yeah, right. Pull the other one. She's not going to sleep with you, just because you say you're dying.

JANICE *(to **WALTER**)* You're being serious, aren't you?

WALTER Afraid so.

DEREK Janice! You're not falling for this, are you?

JANICE *(ignoring **DEREK**)* So what's wrong?

WALTER Nothing much. Just a few dozen diseases attacking me all at once. *(dismissively)* I'll be all right.

JANICE What kind of diseases?

WALTER The kind that give you a dicky heart. The kind that makes you forget things. The kind that kill you. *(picks up the urn and looks at it, longingly)* Inherited from my father, bless him.

JANICE Forget things? At your age?

WALTER What at my age?

JANICE Forget things!

WALTER Who said anything about forgetting things.

JANICE You just said... You're winding me up aren't you? *(WALTER chuckles)* Well, I'm glad that you think it's funny. So, when you say you're dying...

WALTER I mean sooner, rather than later. Weeks rather than months! Doctor Gower says I won't suffer from any serious side-effects until nearer the time. That's why I contacted you. I really did want to get one last 'look in' before I croaked it. Or got too ill to perform. *(he winks at her)*

DEREK Unbelievable!

WALTER Of course I didn't know you had a boyfriend when I rang. If I <u>had</u> known about David, I'd have rescued you from him sooner.

DEREK It's Derek.

JANICE Why me, though? Surely you've been with plenty of girls during your fame.

WALTER You were the only genuine one. I felt I'd not done right by you when we were together. Now that I'm dying, I wanted to find someone I could leave everything to.

JANICE Oh. Well, that's very sweet. But I'm with Derek now, so...

DEREK *(cutting in which a change of attitude)* Err, darling, a quick word in the other room, please. Excuse us a minute, Walter.

DEREK drags JANICE into the dining room. The lights flip over.

JANICE That was a bit rude, Derek. I know you hate the man, but...

DEREK Hate? Hate? Who said hate? I think the guy's just swell.

JANICE But you said...

DEREK Enough about that. I was thinking. Poor Walter. All alone in his final weeks. Maybe you <u>should</u> be with him.

JANICE *(shocked)* What?

DEREK Well, bless him. He's got no one. That's no way to go. He should be with a loved one in the end. <u>I</u> can be with you anytime, but he needs you <u>now</u>.

JANICE What are you saying?

DEREK I'm just saying that, maybe, I get off the scene for a while. You spend some quality time with dear Walter. Whatever you get up to with him, hey, I don't need to know the details. Do what you have to do to make him happy. And then, once the worst happens, you and I resume our love as if nothing happened.

JANICE *(disgusted upon realising what he's suggesting)* And we suddenly become millionaires?

DEREK *(pretending to have only just realised)* Well, I never thought of that, but now that you mention it, he probably would leave you a nice slice of his cash.

JANICE You're sick.

DEREK Hey! I'm just thinking of poor Walter. All alone, no one to hug, no one to hold.

JANICE Of course you are. You're despicable.

DEREK *(turning to WALTER's trophy cabinet)* Look at all the man has achieved. Don't you think he deserves some love at the end?

JANICE Yes, I do. But you're not using me in such a devious way, just to get your hands on a few quid.

DEREK *(scoffs)* It'd be more than a few quid. *(composing himself)* But it's about more than that. It's about helping someone in their hour of need. *(he pulls out a chair)* Everyone will see you as a hero. *(stands on the chair)* They'll say, 'Look! There's that Janice girl that cared for Walter Emerson in his final weeks. *(places his fist across his chest, nobly)* What a fine woman.'

JANICE No... They'll say, 'Look! There's that gold-digger that *(mimes quotations)* "cared" for Walter Emerson in his final weeks. What a tart!'

OLIVIA *(entering SR, to DEREK)* Get the fuck down from there. You'll lose your footing and go arse over tit.

DEREK Sorry. *(climbs down)*

OLIVIA *(looking at the chair seat)* Oh for fucks sake. I've just fucking cleaned that!

DEREK Sorry.

OLIVIA *(starts cleaning the chair)* No fucking respect.

DEREK All right, bloody hell!

JANICE Come on, Derek.

> *JANICE drags DEREK back into the other room. The lights flip back over. DR. GOWER is now also there. He stands in silence looking through some medical charts at the back.*

WALTER Everything all right?

JANICE Yeah, just Derek being an arsehole.

WALTER He sounds terrible. Have I shown you the bedroom yet? It has mirrors on the ceiling. *(indicating the fourth wall)* Daniel, you watch telly or something. We'll just be an hour or so.

DEREK It's Derek! *(advancing towards WALTER)*

JANICE *(holding **DEREK** back)* OK, Walter. You've had your fun. The fact of the matter is. I'm with Daniel now, *(correcting herself)* erm, Derek. So, you'll have to think of someone else, or meet someone new.

WALTER I doubt I have time to meet someone new.

JANICE Why don't you try internet dating?

WALTER But why would I do that? I have hundreds of girls' phone numbers. I could ring any of those and have them round here in minutes.

JANICE But you didn't. You rang me. Because you want something more <u>real</u>. If you try internet dating, you can meet someone completely new. You can leave out all the stuff about you being rich and famous. That way you'll know if the girl likes you, for <u>you</u>.

WALTER I guess.

DEREK But if he leaves all that stuff out, he'll have nothing else going for him.

WALTER That's true. I'll almost be as bad as Dom.

DEREK <u>Derek</u>! You'll almost be as bad as <u>Derek</u>. *(pause)* Wait! *(realising)*

JANICE Have you got a computer?

WALTER My laptop's just by the side of the sofa.

*He points past her, towards the side of the sofa. **JANICE** grabs the laptop and sits on the sofa. Suddenly, dread appears on **WALTER**'s face.*

WALTER WAIT!

*Too late. **JANICE** opens up the laptop. The sound of a pornographic video is heard for a few moments before **WALTER** snatches the laptop and quickly shuts off the video.*

JANICE Walter!

WALTER *(handing her the laptop back)* Ha-ha, don't mind that. Just a bit of research.

DEREK If you need to watch videos like that for tips, maybe I <u>don't</u> have anything to worry about.

WALTER I think your girlfriend would confirm that I never needed any help in <u>that</u> department.

JANICE *(sniggering)* Walter!

WALTER *(teasingly)* Remember that summer. At Peace Park? When we did that-thing-with-the-thing-on-the-thing?

JANICE *(responding in kind)* Oh, that-thing-with-the-thing-on-thing.

DEREK *(snapping)* I'm right here!

JANICE *(sniggering)* Sorry, Derek, love.

OLIVIA *(entering from the dining room)* There, all clean. *(spotting **DEREK**)* I hope you haven't come to trample on all the furniture in here as well. If God wanted you airborne he'd have given you wings, like he gave me a duster and polish. *(to **WALTER**)* You wanna watch this one Mr. Emerson. This fucking moronic idiot *(indicating **DEREK**)* has dragged muddy footprints all through the house. *(heads to the back of the room to clean)*

WALTER I see you've already met Olivia. My cleaner!

JANICE We have indeed. Her language is quite colourful.

WALTER Olivia's a classy lady I'll have you know.

OLIVIA *(she farts)* 'scuse me!

JANICE Yes. I can see that.

OLIVIA *(farts again)* Oooooh. *(laughs)* More tea vicar?

WALTER *(to **OLIVIA**)* Speaking of tea, why don't you make our guests a cuppa.

OLIVIA Go on then.

WALTER I'll have the usual, please.

OLIVIA looks at JANICE for her order.

JANICE Black coffee, please.

DEREK I'll have a coffee, too, please. Milk, one sugar.

OLIVIA exits SL.

JANICE Right! Let's get to work. *(starts typing on the laptop)* It's never been easier to meet new people. *(after a few moments of typing)* Ok, here we go, this a good site.

DEREK How do you know?

JANICE Oh, I was, erm, using it for a bit… Last year.

DEREK Oh. *(realising after a brief pause)* Last year? We started seeing each other <u>two</u> years ago.

JANICE Did we? Oh. Sorry, I meant two years ago.

DEREK Janice!

JANICE Lighten up, Derek. I'm just winding you up. *(**WALTER** laughs)* Ok. Let's build you a profile.

DEREK Start with, obnoxious, ignorant, arrogant, self-absorbed.
JANICE We're not doing yours!

WALTER laughs again as JANICE continues typing. After a few moments, WALTER points at something that JANICE just typed.

WALTER That's a good one.

DEREK gives the pair an annoyed look. After bit more typing DEREK points at something that JANICE just typed.

DEREK How do you know that?
WALTER *(smiling)* You remembered! *(WALTER and JANICE chuckle)*
DEREK OK. Can you two knock it off now, please?
JANICE *(finishes typing)* Done.

A message tone is heard from the laptop.

WALTER What was that?
JANICE You've got a message.
DEREK That was fast!
WALTER What does it say?
JANICE "Thank you for joining Love Finder Online. Please read our terms and..."
WALTER Well that's disappointing. Where are the girls?
JANICE Give it time. I've only just created your profile.
WALTER It's because you didn't tell them that I'm loaded.
JANICE It's because it's only been ten seconds.
WALTER *(takes control of the laptop and begins typing)* Let's just pop in the fact that I'm rich. The girls love it.
JANICE I don't know how shallow you think we are, but...

JANICE is interrupted by a series of message tones.

WALTER Now we're talking.
JANICE Nope *(takes back control of the laptop and types)*. Delete.
WALTER Hey!
JANICE You're not messaging any of those girls. *(she looks closer at the screen)* Or... or this guy. And I'm deleting the stuff you just added. We're waiting for someone more genuine than that.
WALTER Can't I just search for them?

JANICE I suppose, but we need to input some filters to find someone who will match with you.

WALTER I can't be bothered messing about with that. I just want to get my leg over.

DR. GOWER *(looking up from his papers)* 'Get your leg over'?

WALTER You know, *(thrusting hips again)* get my leg over.

DEREK *(to WALTER)* How long has the butler been stood back there?

DR. GOWER I have a doctorate.

DEREK Then why are you working as a butler?

DR. GOWER *(annoyed)* I am not a…

WALTER Hush now, Alfred.

OLIVIA *(entering SL with three cups)* Here's your fucking drinks you bone idle lazy bastards.

WALTER, JANICE and DEREK take one each.

DEREK Thanks. *(takes a sip and spits it back out)* What the hell is this? *(looking into his cup)*

OLIVIA Well we was out of coffee, so I used gravy granules instead.

WALTER laughs and the three of them put their cups down. OLIVIA resumes her cleaning exiting SL at some point as she goes about this.

WALTER I guess we'll have tea then if we're all out of coffee. Doctor Gower! Maybe <u>you</u> could take care of it instead, please?

DR. GOWER I'm the doctor. Not the tea boy.

WALTER But my <u>health</u> will be so much better after a cup of tea.

DR. GOWER *(sinister)* Very well, I'll make you a tea. I'll make you a tea you'll never forget. *(grabs the cups)* What's everyone having?

WALTER Milk, one sugar, please.

JANICE Same, please.

DEREK And again, thanks.

DR. GOWER starts to leave.

WALTER Wait. Doctor, doctor. I've just swallowed a roll of film.

DR. GOWER Well, let's wait until morning and see what develops.

WALTER Damn it!

DR. GOWER Why not try a butler joke? You'd catch me out with one of those. *(exits SL)*

JANICE What was that about?

WALTER *(dismissively)* Just a thing we do. Anyway, come on. Find me someone.

JANICE Well what are you looking for?

WALTER Female.

JANICE *(long pause)* Yes, go on.

WALTER Go on what? That's it. Just bring up the first two girls that you find.

JANICE Two?

WALTER Well I can't put all my eggs in one basket, can I?

JANICE But what if they're not into the same things as you?

WALTER So? I'll fake interest.

JANICE *(defeated)* Fine! *(typing)* OK. First girl. Fran Phillips.

WALTER She'll do.

JANICE *(looks up at **WALTER** for a moment before rolling her eyes and looking back at the screen)* She's looking to meet a 'proper' gentleman with old fashioned values. She loves swimming and cycling. Oh, she's won some squash tournaments, that's impressive. Sounds like she's into her fitness. And her art. *(showing **WALTER** the screen)* Look! There's a list of all the famous galleries that she's visited. *(looking back to the screen)* What else... *(continuing reading)* It says she's very superstitious. Vegan.

DEREK *(rolling his eyes)* Oh, God! One of them.

JANICE *(continuing without acknowledging his comment)* Cares for the environment and wants to meet someone who shares her passions.

WALTER I'll take her.

JANICE Oh dear!

WALTER *(takes over the typing)* Ok, now just to...

JANICE *(confused)* What are you doing?

WALTER *(still typing)* Just ordering a few swimming and cycling trophies.

DEREK You wouldn't.

JANICE He would.

WALTER It's good to have some supporting material if I'm going to feign interest. That's those ordered. Oh, and whilst I'm at it, I'll print off a fake certificate. *(thinking before typing)* Let's go with, 'Eco Warrior of the Year'. *(remembering)* There's that thing about art, too. *(thinking)* I know! Doctor Gower has a fancy painting in his office upstairs. I'll hang that in dining room so that she sees it when she comes in. That should impress her.

JANICE You're unbelievable. You don't even know if you'll get a date with her yet.

WALTER I like to be optimistic. Right, onto the next girl.

JANICE *(typing)* OK. *(reading the screen)* Zara Cooper. She describes herself as a spunky girl. Always up for a laugh. Her ideal man would have tattoos, piercings, long hair and own a motorbike. *(looking up)* Sounds like she's into bad boys. *(glancing back at the screen)* Oh and it says she's scared of dogs.

WALTER Add to basket! One of these girls are likely to pan out.

JANICE But these two are nothing alike. And you're nothing like either of the men these two women want to meet.

WALTER So? I only have to pretend long enough to seal the deal!

JANICE Seal the deal?

WALTER *(thrusting his hips once per word)* Seal. The. Deal.

JANICE You don't really think you can pull this off, do you? Use alter egos in an attempt to impress these girls into bed.

WALTER I did a bit of am dram at school. Shouldn't be too tricky.

JANICE But it wouldn't be fair to either of them. You'd just be faking it.

WALTER I've been with enough women to know they have no problem doing that to me. Just send the messages.

OLIVIA re-enters from SL, still cleaning various things as she does.

JANICE Fine. We'll need a different picture of you. Well two pictures, actually. One for each girl, because you're going to need to look different for both.

WALTER No problem. We'll sort that out later.

*At this point **OLIVIA** is dusting the shelf with the urn on it when she glances at the laptop screen from across the room. She is holding the urn very carelessly.*

OLIVIA Aw! Look at her. She's as cute as a bug's ear.

WALTER Olivia please be careful with that. It's got my father's ashes in it.

OLIVIA I'm just giving it the once over. *(she carries on dusting the shelf whilst holding the urn haphazardly to one side)*

WALTER *(worried)* Well try not to spill him.

OLIVIA *(turning to address him and motioning, carelessly, with the urn as she speaks, causing **WALTER** to cringe with each sharp movement)* Oh you're right to be worried. Barbara, this old bat that I clean for, had her urn knocked off the mantle at her house. It's what had her husband in, as well. His ashes went everywhere. There was no getting him back in.

WALTER How did she take it?

OLIVIA She never found out. I just scooped out the bottom of the fireplace, re-filled the urn and put it back like nothing had happened.

WALTER Wait… It was you that knocked it off?

OLIVIA Oh yes. I was worried shitless that she'd find out.

WALTER *(rushing over and grabbing the urn)* Why don't I just take this, and you go and clean the bedroom or something

OLIVIA Fair enough.

*OLIVIA exits SL passing **DR. GOWER** who enters with three identical looking cups of tea on a tray. He is also now wearing a black tuxedo with a bow tie. **WALTER** returns the urn to the shelf.*

DR. GOWER Tea, sir.

WALTER Why are you wearing a suit? *(realising with dread)* Is that from my collection?

DR. GOWER It's not just any suit. Here's your tea, sir. *(in Sean Connery's voice)* Shaken, not stirred.

WALTER Not my Bond tux.

DR. GOWER That's right. I felt if you were going to treat me like a butler, then I should start to look the part. 007 at your service.

WALTER *(serious)* This isn't funny, Doc. That thing's priceless! You do know it's the actual one he wore in the movies, right?

DEREK It's very sharp.

WALTER Between you and Olivia my blood pressure will be through the roof. Put it back right now, before you ruin it.

DR. GOWER *(rolls his eyes)* Very well. Take your teas first.

WALTER reaches for a cup.

DR. GOWER Not that one! That one's yours. *(pointing to a different cup)*

WALTER We all asked for milk, one sugar. They're all the same.

DR. GOWER No they're not.

WALTER *(surveying him for a moment before taking it)* You're bluffing.

DR. GOWER Then you have nothing to worry about, do you?

DEREK Which one's mine?

DR. GOWER Any of the others, sir. They're both the same.

DEREK takes a cup and places it down. DR. GOWER heads over to JANICE and stands over her.

DR. GOWER Your tea, madam.
JANICE *(busy typing)* Two seconds. I think one of the girls has replied already.
DEREK Really? *(looks at the screen)*

WALTER uses this opportunity to swap cups with DEREK.

JANICE Really! I just need to find the message. Here it is.
WALTER Well? What did she say?
JANICE I've got you a date! For tonight! Just call me cupid, ladies and gentlemen.

JANICE stands up and bows, throwing her arms to the side, knocking the tray with the tea all over DR. GOWER. WALTER goes berserk.

WALTER No! My suit!
JANICE Walter, I'm so sorry.
WALTER *(shouting at DR. GOWER)* This is what you get for messing around!
DR. GOWER *(looking worried)* Walter I'm really… I didn't know that… Well I didn't think that… *(giving up)* Oh, what do you care. You'll be dead soon anyway.
OLIVIA Quick! Into the kitchen. I'll soak it in the basin. *(she takes DR.GOWER off SL)*
WALTER *(as he follows them off SL)* Don't make it any worse!
JANICE *(to DEREK)* Oops.
DEREK I'm sure it'll come out.
JANICE I was really looking forward to that brew, too.
DEREK *(picks his up)* Here. You can have mine.
JANICE Aw. Thanks, Derek, love. *(takes a big gulp)*

Blackout.

Act 1 Scene 2 - Fran's First Date

Lights come up in the living room, only. DEREK is laid on the sofa watching television. JANICE is pacing up and down. OLIVIA is cleaning.

JANICE *(shouting off SL)* Walter! Hurry up, she'll be here soon.

DEREK What's the matter with you? Walter's the one who should be nervous.

JANICE I'm excited for him. I just want everything to work out OK.

OLIVIA *(to **DEREK**)* Is your washing machine broken, or are you just saving water?

DEREK What do you mean?

OLIVIA They look like you've slept in em. *(points at a stain on his clothes)* Looks like you've got half of yesterdays breakfast on ya.

DEREK They're clean on today!

JANICE You little liar. You wore them to my mothers house last night.

OLIVIA I can practically smell the salmonella on ya.

WALTER *(entering SL in a suit)* Well? How do I look?

JANICE Like a true gentleman.

WALTER So, my tailor did a good job then?

DEREK You have your own tailor?

DR. GOWER *(entering in a grey suit with a yellow measuring tape in his hand)* What do you think?

DEREK I'm actually impressed you've got a date so soon. Which one was it?

JANICE It's Fran Phillips. The posh one.

DEREK Oh yeah. The swimmer, slash, cyclist, slash, squash player.

JANICE That's her. <u>And</u> I managed to get him a date with the other one for tomorrow night.

WALTER Really? You're better at being me, than me!

OLIVIA Walter, I've cleaned the dining room. There was a box on the table. I wasn't sure what it was, so I left it.

WALTER Don't worry about that. They're my props for tonight.

OLIVIA Oh, all right. Well I've given your trophies and things a good polish. They've come up all shiny like a new pin. I could see my face in 'em, my whiskers and everything. I spent hours on the things.

WALTER Oh! Well you needn't have bothered. I'll be taking them down before the date and swapping them out with different ones.

OLIVIA Oh well that's fucking brilliant that is! You could have said something before I'd polished them to within an inch of their lives. It wasn't a pleasant experience when I got a glimpse of a moustached man in the reflection in the brass. Turns out my nose hair had just got a bit out of hand.

WALTER Well at least they're done for when I put them back up.

OLIVIA 'Spose I'll go outside and get on with the gutters. *(exits SR).*

DR. GOWER Speaking of which. How are your guts?

WALTER *(looking suspicious)* Fine… Why are you asking that?

DR. GOWER *(confused)* Hmm. It should have kicked in by now.

WALTER *(whispering)* If you genuinely did put something in my drink I'll be fine. I swapped cups with Derek.

DR. GOWER *(matching his volume)* Oh dear. In that case, I'd get him off the sofa then.

WALTER I'm proud of you, Doc. I didn't think you had it in you. *(looks at his watch)* Anyway, shouldn't you be getting ready?

DR. GOWER rolls his eyes and exits SL

JANICE *(grabbing DEREK's hand with the intention of leaving)* We'll leave you to it then.

WALTER Oh no you don't. You got me into this mess, you can stick around in case I need help.

JANICE Won't she find that a bit weird? The two of us crashing your date?

WALTER You won't be crashing the date. You can stay in here and watch us through the CCTV on the laptop.

JANICE You have a security camera in the dining room?

WALTER I have hidden cameras in every room of the house.

JANICE OK. We'll stay. I'll keep her profile page open on the laptop, so if you need a refresher, you can excuse yourself and come in here.

WALTER Good idea. Just make sure you're quiet in here. Wish me luck.

JANICE Good luck!

WALTER heads into the dining room, leaving JANICE and DEREK huddled on the sofa with the laptop. The lights swap over. There is a Monet painting hanging on the wall now. A small bell and a large cardboard box are on the dining room table. WALTER takes out the contents; a few trophies and some framed certificates. He walks over to his actual awards and shoves them all into this box before replacing them with his fake ones. The doorbell rings. WALTER exits SR with the box in hand. He returns without the box, followed by FRAN. WALTER puts on a posh voice throughout his time with FRAN.

WALTER Hello madam. *(taking a bow)* Walter Emerson. What at an absolute pleasure it is to meet you. *(kisses her hand)*

FRAN Oh, how courteous. Fran Phillips. But you already knew that. *(looking around, amazed)*

WALTER So, did you find me OK?

FRAN I did, but I was sure that I must have taken a wrong turn. I checked and double checked the address before calling on you. You never said in your messages that you lived in a mansion.

WALTER Well I'm not one to show off. *(he says this as he leans on his trophy shelf, very obviously)*

FRAN You have quite the trophy collection. *(picking one up)* You didn't tell me you played squash.

WALTER Oh, that old thing. Won that when I did a tour of Switzerland playing for a European league. I remember the final like it was yesterday. I played so hard that I broke my bat.

FRAN Your what?

WALTER You know. What you hit the ball with.

FRAN A racket?

WALTER Yes, it was pretty noisy. The stadium was packed. *(realising and panicking)* Oh… Of course… The racket... Ha-ha… I knew that, yes. It's just in Switzerland they called them bats.

FRAN They do? How peculiar. I never knew that. *(picking up another trophy)* Oh, you have one for cycling too. Le Tour de France!

WALTER No, I got that one in England.

FRAN *(awkwardly)* I see. My friend and I would quarrel for hours over who has the better bike; The better make, the best brand of tyre. Which is the best type of clip! Do you have some good cycling clips?

WALTER No, there was no one filming me when I did it, so we haven't got any footage.

FRAN *(staring at him wide-eyed)* No, I meant clips, dear. Like what holds your shoe to the pedal.

WALTER Oh clips! Yes of course. Sorry. Ha-ha. Silly moment there.

FRAN What brand are you using? Because I find that also makes all the difference.

WALTER Oh, well, you know. I find that a good old household peg does the trick.

FRAN *(starts laughing)* You <u>are</u> funny. *(picking up the next trophy)* Oh. Swimming too. *(studying all the trophies again)* You know... You have a trophy in all the sports I listed as hobbies on my profile. What a coincidence.

WALTER *(fanning his shirt)* Yes… Coincidence.

FRAN I'm not actually a great swimmer myself. I can only swim breaststroke. How about you?

WALTER *(aside)* I think I might have a stroke at this rate.

FRAN *(she gets a text on her phone)* Sorry about this. I don't wish to appear rude, but my friends have asked me to check in with them regularly. They do worry, bless them. They really wanted me to go on this date, but found it rather peculiar that you wanted the first date to be at your house. You said in your message that there was some sort of reason why we couldn't go out?

WALTER Yes, I don't really want to go into it, but I have a little illness. Nothing serious, but I need to be close to my doctor at all times.

FRAN Your doctor is here now?

WALTER Yes, but don't worry. He mostly keeps to himself.

FRAN I see. *(spotting a coin collection display case on his shelf)* My word. What a lovely collection of coins. Fifteenth century if I'm not mistaken.

WALTER *(surprised)* That's right! How did you know?

FRAN I'm somewhat of a collector myself.

WALTER Really? There was no mention of that in your profile.

FRAN I didn't want people to think I was strange. *(spotting the antique weapons)* They're rather nice too. I imagine they're worth a bit.

WALTER *(picking one up)* This one alone sells for half a million.

FRAN Really? That's ludicrous. And, what about the vases? They look really old.

WALTER Just material things I picked up on my travels. I'm not actually sure of their value.

FRAN *(indicating the painting)* Monet?

WALTER Seven or Eight thousand I believe it was.

FRAN *(laughing at what she thinks is a joke)* Oh you are a card. You must think me terribly boring. *(her phone receives another text)* Oh, sorry about this. *(checking it again)*

WALTER Don't worry about it. It's understandable for your friends to be concerned, this day and age. *(drawing a chair for her)* Why don't you take a seat and I'll see how dinner is coming along.

FRAN Thank you, Walter. *(taking a seat at the dinner table)*

WALTER heads into the living room side of the stage and the lights come up. FRAN continues to use her phone. JANICE and DEREK both look up at WALTER from the sofa when he enters. WALTER resumes his normal accent whilst talking to these two.

DEREK "I find that a good old household peg does the trick?" Are you for real?

WALTER I had no idea what she was talking about.

JANICE And the painting is by the artist "Monet" you wally. But I think it's fine. She thought you were joking.

DEREK Either way, I think it'll take months to get this one in the sack.

WALTER I don't have months!

JANICE We don't know that. Stay positive. *(looking at laptop screen)* She's texting on her phone quite a lot. She's probably writing about you. You could see how the date was going if you get a hold of that phone.

WALTER I can't do that. It's immoral. I'd be racked with guilt.

DEREK Well it's not like you'll have to live with it for long.

WALTER I'm starting to think it's only OK for <u>me</u> to joke about my coming demise.

JANICE It's just a suggestion.

WALTER Fine, I'll try. If I get chance.

OLIVIA enters SR. Her hands covered in sludge and dead leaves.

JANICE *(looking at the laptop)* Oh no!

WALTER What is it?

JANICE Your cleaner's in there.

Lights go down on the living room.

OLIVIA Fuck me! It's bloody freezing out there. I'm fucking nithered. It's a good job I'm not a brass monkey.

FRAN Good heavens.

OLIVIA It's blowing a gale out there. It blew my frock over my head whilst I was up the ladders. Thank fuck for knitted tights. The neighbour was out there washing his car too. I hope he wasn't traumatised by my arse.

FRAN Who on earth are you?

OLIVIA 'names Olivia. Am the cleaner. *(holds her hand out)*

FRAN *(looking at her dirty hand)* Oh. Erm. Charmed. *(refuses to shake hands with her)*

OLIVIA Them gutters are fucking filthy. I've got crap all over my Primani coat! *(goes to hang it up on the coat stand next to FRAN's coat)*

FRAN NO!

FRAN leaps up and grabbing her own coat so that it doesn't touch OLIVIA's. She puts her own coat safely on the back of her chair and OLIVIA hangs hers on the coat stand.

FRAN Looks like you've been busy. *(indicating her filthy arms)*

OLIVIA Oh this is nothing. I clean for some of the old 'uns at Midgely Retirement Home. I spent my morning cleaning up shit and piss. Oh, and one of 'em, Beatrice, died this morning. Well, I didn't want her lying dead in a mucky flat, so I cleaned up around her. I felt really uncomfortable. I'm sure she was looking at me.

FRAN And the staff were happy for you to do that? Carry on cleaning whilst she just lay there, deceased?

OLIVIA They didn't even know she was dead. So, I finished up my cleaning and mentioned it to someone on my way out.

FRAN Oh my!

OLIVIA I must have been doing a good job for her though. She's left me a load of old tat in her will.

FRAN What kind of old tat?

OLIVIA Some old china. Ornaments. You know, old lady shite.

FRAN Some of it may not just be tat. You should let me look it over. I'll let you know if any of it's worth something.

OLIVIA Got a good eye for that sort of thing, do ya?

FRAN I know a little about the market, yes. I'd be happy to cast an eye over it for you.

OLIVIA I might just take you up on that! It was only the other day that Sylvia died! I cleaned for her too. And Patricia, another one, she's looking a bit worse for wear as well, now. Won't be long till she's gone, I reckon. Putting me out of work this lot; fucking dying all the time. That's why I'm glad I've got this job. I can't imagine a young man like Walter's gonna die anytime soon.

WALTER *(enters the dining room)* Olivia! Why don't you go to the kitchen and get cleaned up?

OLIVIA Aye. I best had. Oh, Walter. Whilst I've got you. I could use a few bits. I shouldn't be cleaning the gutter with my hands.

WALTER OK. Just give me a list of your expenses and I'll give you the money.

OLIVIA Oh good. *(pulls out a piece of paper and starts reading)* I need some new flannels, cream cleaner, furniture polish, mildew remover, some new mop heads, all-natural pine cleaner. I need some funding to tackle dust creation.

WALTER Dust creation?

OLIVIA Oh yes. They don't fund it up at Midgely Retirement home. Them folks must be swimming in dead skin cells.

WALTER OK. I'll sort you out with some money later.

OLIVIA I'll go and get washed up. *(exits SL)*

FRAN So how is it?

WALTER How is what?

FRAN Dinner!

WALTER Dinner? Oh dinner! Yes. I should probably find out.

FRAN I thought that's where you went.

WALTER I did? Oh, I mean, I did yes. It's fine.

FRAN Would you like some help? I'm quite the culinary artiste myself, you know.

WALTER Oh not at all. You're my guest. Besides. The chef is taking care of everything.

FRAN You have your own chef?

WALTER Oh yes.

> *WALTER grabs the bell from the table and gives it a little ring.*
> *DR. GOWER enters wearing a chef's hat and apron. He has a meal on a plate in each hand.*

DR. GOWER You rang, sir?

WALTER Yes. We're ready to eat now, Alejandro.

> *DR. GOWER gives him a sarcastic look and places a meal in front of each of them.*

FRAN Oh this looks wonderful, Chef. And you did the vegan option for me, too. Thank you very much.

DR. GOWER I have a doctorate. *(spotting the painting)* Is that my…

WALTER That'll be all, chef.

> *WALTER gestures for him to leave with a couple of flicks of his hand.*
> *DR. GOWER exits after giving WALTER a stern look.*

FRAN I could certainly get used to this lifestyle. Would you mind if I freshen up before we eat?

WALTER Not at all. The toile… err… the restroom, is just back towards the front door, and right down the corridor. *(pointing off SR)* It's the first door on the left.

FRAN Thank you.

FRAN stands and exits SR, leaving her phone behind on the table.
WALTER whistles for a moment before spotting the phone. He has a
brief internal struggle with his morals and then grabs the phone. He
taps the screen a few times.

WALTER Bollocks.

He moves into the living room. The lights flip over.

JANICE What's wrong?
WALTER It's locked! *(points at the laptop)* Quick, rewind the footage
   and try and see what code she types in.
DEREK Got over your moral dilemma, then?
JANICE *(checking the laptop to find the code)* Looks like... Three, Five,
   Nine, Nine.
WALTER Thanks. *(he inputs the code)* Oh? *(he smirks at what he sees)*
JANICE What is it?
WALTER *(smirks)* Nothing for you to worry about, Janice... *(lights
   begin to fade on his last sentence)* Nothing at all.

Blackout.

Act 1 Scene 3 - Zara's First Date

*A day passes. Lights come up on the living room. **DEREK** is sat on the*
*sofa watching television again and **JANICE** is pacing up and down*
*again. **OLIVIA** is mopping the floor.*

JANICE *(shouting off SL)* Walter! Hurry up! She'll be here soon.
DEREK Calm down, Janice.
JANICE I can't. I'm too nervous. *(holding her stomach)* It's upsetting
   my stomach.
DEREK What's this one like again?
JANICE The one that wants the bad boy. Tattoos, piercings, long hair,
   all that kind of stuff.
DEREK So everything that Walter isn't then?
JANICE Hence, me being nervous.
OLIVIA *(to DEREK)* Didn't you have those same clothes on yesterday
   when you were here.
DEREK Erm... No...

JANICE See! I told you someone would notice.

DEREK Relax. They've been washed.

JANICE No they haven't.

DEREK How do you know?

JANICE Cause I'm the one that does the washing.

OLIVIA You should take pride in your appearance, you little scrote.

DEREK *(sniffing himself)* They've got another couple of days in them, yet.

OLIVIA You fucking scruff! They want running through the wash.

WALTER enters SL. He is wearing jeans, a 'wife-beater' vest and a long-haired wig.

DEREK *(laughing hoarsely)* No way! I am not seeing this.

JANICE That's it. That's the look.

WALTER Really? I feel stupid.

DEREK If it's any consolation. You look it.

WALTER At least I have to add things to my appearance to look stupid. You get there all on your own. *(to JANICE)* Can I lose the wig?

JANICE No. That's what you were wearing in the picture you sent her, so it's gonna have to stay. Can you remember what she likes? We don't want any mistakes this time.

WALTER Yes. Bad boy. *(puts on a 'bad-boy' voice and adjusts his stance)* You wouldn't want to bump into me in a dark alley.

WALTER kicks OLIVIA's mop bucket by mistake during this.

OLIVIA Go steady, Walter. Don't kick the bucket.

WALTER If only it were that easy, Olivia.

JANICE *(noticing his bare arms)* Tattoos! Where are the tattoos?

WALTER Doctor Gower's just grabbing it for me now.

DEREK It? You're not using one of those fake sleeve things, are you?

JANICE She won't know.

DEREK Of course she will.

DR. GOWER *(enters SL with the fake tattoo sleeve)* Here it is. Hold out your arm, Walter.

WALTER holds his arm out and DR. GOWER rolls the fake tattoo sleeve up his arm. WALTER looks at the first tattoo in shock.

WALTER A unicorn?

DR. GOWER What's wrong with that?

WALTER Well it doesn't exactly scream 'danger' does it?

DR. GOWER Well there's a skull and cross bone, some barbed wire and a motorbike on there too. What more do you want?

WALTER Ideally not a girly unicorn.

JANICE Remember to change your attitude, too. None of that posh stuff that you did with Fran.

WALTER I know.

DEREK How did things end up going with her?

WALTER Not bad actually. She said she would see me again and we've messaged each other a few times, so I just need to arrange another date.

The doorbell rings.

WALTER She's here. Quick!

JANICE It's fine. Make her wait a bit. She'll love it.

WALTER What?

JANICE Trust me. *(her stomach groans and she grabs at it)* Urgh.

DEREK Are you OK?

JANICE Yeah. Just a bit of an upset tummy. You know, I've not felt right since you gave me your cuppa when we were here yesterday.

***DR. GOWER** and **WALTER** give each other a look of realisation. The doorbell rings again.*

WALTER Doctor! Grab my stuff. *(**DR. GOWER** sighs and starts to head off)* Oh, and, doctor, doctor. I'm addicted to brake fluid.

DR. GOWER Nonsense, you can stop any time. *(exits SL)*

WALTER Dammit.

DEREK He's good.

***DR. GOWER** returns with some biker leathers and a helmet. The doorbell rings several times, rapidly. **WALTER** puts his biker outfit on.*

JANICE Good luck! We'll be watching. *(pointing at the laptop)*

***WALTER** moves to the other room. The lights flip over. There's another box on the table. **WALTER** swaps the trophies and certificates again with the ones in the box. He exits SR, with the box again, to*

*answer the door. He returns, without the box, followed by **ZARA**.*
***WALTER** speaks in a gruff, cocky voice whenever **ZARA** is present.*

WALTER Sorry I took so long answering the door. I literally just got back from jumping twenty trucks on my motorbike.

ZARA I didn't think you were going to answer. I nearly sacked it off. It's bloody freezing out there.

WALTER Oh no. I hope you're not... I mean... err... you'll be right. It's only a bit of cold.

ZARA Aye, I suppose. At least it's nice and warm in here.

*   **ZARA** turns her back to **WALTER** and begins to look around the dining room. **WALTER** removes his helmet, accidentally catching his wig with it, knocking it to fall to the floor.*

ZARA Bitchin' pad you got here. This place is massive.
WALTER *(panicking)* Yeah... it's err... all right I suppose.

*   **WALTER** manages to get his wig back on moments before she turns around.*

ZARA Wow! I love your hair. I mean, I loved it on the photos, but it looks way cooler in person. Can I run my fingers through it?

WALTER Yeah. Go for it. *(she approaches)* I MEAN NO! NO! *(she freezes)* I mean, well, we've only just met. It'd be a bit weird. *(he takes his biker leathers off)*

ZARA All right. Sorry. *(spotting his tattoos)* Cool tats. *(taking his arm and studying them)* Motorbike, of course!

WALTER Yeah! The design is based on my actual bike.

ZARA Nice! *(looking at more tattoos)* Cool skull and... Is that a unicorn?

WALTER Yes, yes it is. It's to show that I'm horny. *(**ZARA** goes wide-eyed)* I mean... *(realising what he said)* Not horny as in, like horny, like that. I meant sharp and pointy. Like I have a nice big point. *(**ZARA** goes wide-eyed again)* I mean...*(realising again)* Not that I mean that I have a large point... more like... I MEAN... NOT THAT I HAVE A SMALL POINT BY ANY MEANS. I... *(giving up)* His name is Damien the mean unicorn.

ZARA Aw bless ya. Ya nervous.

WALTER Oh God. Sorry. What about you? I expected you to have loads of tattoos.

ZARA Oh I have. It's just err... not appropriate to show you them on the first date. Maybe next time. *(she winks and walks away, leaving him stunned)*

WALTER *(nervously)* Ha... ha... I just need to... err... nip next door for a minute. Make yourself comfortable. I'll go and get dinner. Excuse me, please.

ZARA sits at the table and WALTER exits to the other room. The lights flip over.

DEREK You, my friend, are dying out there. And I don't mean literally.

WALTER It's all going wrong.

DR. GOWER It's all going right for me. I have the cameras set to record. I'm looking at a good two million hits online when I upload this.

JANICE You're being too nice. "Make yourself comfortable?" "Excuse me, please." No, no, no. That's all wrong. This isn't Fran out there. You need to adjust. Get her name wrong, or something.

WALTER OK, I'll try harder.

DR. GOWER *(to JANICE)* Well he handled the cooking himself tonight, so he may end up poisoning her. Is that more 'Zara appropriate?'

JANICE Maybe a bit too far, that.

DR. GOWER I'm almost at a loss being required to only do my <u>actual</u> job tonight.

WALTER I could do with a gardener! The neighbour's cat has shit on my lawn again.

DR. GOWER Quick reminder... Doctor... Not gardener.

WALTER But if I go out there and deal with it, it may very well impact my health. So you would still be providing a medical service.

DR. GOWER *(sighs)* And what exactly would you like me to do about said neighbour's feline faeces?

WALTER Go and get a spade and chuck it over into <u>their</u> garden.

DR. GOWER *(with a twinkle in his eye)* Very well. I shall do just that. *(exits SL)*

WALTER OK. *(to himself)* Dinner time. *(exits SL)*

DEREK Do you know how to tell the difference between an alligator and a crocodile. *(JANICE simply looks at him for the answer)* You can tell based on if they see you later or in a while...

JANICE doesn't laugh, she simply gives him a sympathetic look. WALTER returns with a steak dinner on a plate and a bowl of soup.

WALTER OK, I'm going back in.

JANICE Remember; Treat em mean, keep em keen.

WALTER Treat em mean, keep em keen. Got it!

WALTER enters the dining room. The lights flip over. He places the meal in front of the empty chair.

ZARA Nice! Steak. That looks yummy.

WALTER Here's ya soup, ya bitch!

WALTER places the bowl in front of her and throws the spoon in causing the soup to splash all over her.

ZARA Are you taking the piss?

WALTER Tuck in.

WALTER takes a seat and starts to eat his meal. ZARA begins to eat her soup. There is a long silence.

ZARA This is quite nice, actually. Did you make it yourself?

WALTER It's out of a tin.

ZARA Oh. *(another long silence)* So, your bike. I'd love to see it. Maybe you could take me for a ride on it?

WALTER I don't know about that. The last girl I took out on it fell off the back. It was her own fault so I just carried on. Ain't no one ruining my ride.

ZARA Ruthless!

WALTER How did you know her name was Ruth?

ZARA *(laughs)* I promise I'll hold on <u>real</u> tight.

WALTER Oh... err... Well... I can't, anyway. It's broken.

ZARA But you just said you jumped twenty trucks on it.

WALTER Well yes. <u>I</u> did, but my bike only made it over nineteen of them.

ZARA Woah! Are you OK?

WALTER Oh yeah. Happens all the time. Just the odd scrape. I'm tough so it's nothing to me.

DR. GOWER enters SR wearing a gardening apron. He dumps a pair of gardening gloves on the table causing ZARA to jump.

ZARA Oh, you scared me.

WALTER This is my gardener, Antwon.

DR. GOWER I have a doctorate.

WALTER Did you do what I asked?

DR. GOWER Yes, but I don't know what it has achieved. Now the neighbour has our spade and there's still cat shit in the garden.

WALTER What?

DR. GOWER You said to get a spade and chuck it into the neighbour's garden.

WALTER I meant the cat poop, you buffoon.

DR. GOWER You should have been more specific.

ZARA laughs. **DR. GOWER** *grabs the gloves and returns to the living room where the lights are still down.*

WALTER That man!

As she eats her soup, **ZARA** *looks around the room. She spots a framed photo on the shelf. She heads over and picks it up.*

ZARA Aw. This is cool. You and Steve McQueen. He's one of my all-time favourite bikers. Who did this for you?

WALTER Did it?

ZARA Yeah, you know, photo-shopped it. It looks proper genuine.

WALTER It is genuine. Me and Steve go way back. He lets me call him 'Stevie'. What a guy. I'd introduce you, but he's on holiday. Peru. Don't tell the paparazzi.

ZARA Steve McQueen died in nineteen-eighty.

WALTER *(long pause)* I know that. Ha-ha. I'm just winding you up. I have an 'idiot' friend called DEREK. *(shouting towards the other room)* He's good with computers. He did it for me. Too bad he's a complete ARSEHOLE. *(to the other room again)*

The lights flip over briefly. **DEREK** *and* **DR. GOWER** *are laughing.* **JANICE** *doesn't look amused.*

JANICE You did that photo? And you didn't tell him he was dead?

DEREK Oh come on, that was priceless.

DR. GOWER *gives* **DEREK** *a high-five. The lights flip back over.*

ZARA It's still pretty cool. Do you think he'd do me one?

WALTER Yeah, I could ask him if you wa... I mean... No! Get your own friends. Jeez.

ZARA All right. Calm down.

WALTER *(flustered)* I'll just go check on the dessert. I'll be right back, Stephanie.

ZARA ... It's Zara...

WALTER *(too obvious)* Oh, sorry. My mistake.

ZARA Don't be long.

WALTER I'll be as long as it takes.

WALTER moves to the living room. The lights flip over.

WALTER *(pointing at **DEREK**)* Scumbag!

JANICE Stephanie? When I said get her name wrong, I meant for it to sound something similar at least. You know... Zandra... Zoe... That sort of thing! What are you doing in here anyway? Get back in there.

WALTER I can't. It's too hard to be this confrontational all the time. I'm surprised she hasn't left yet.

JANICE You're doing fine. "I'll be as long as it takes" was perfect! Go on. Go back to her!

WALTER Gimme a minute. I need a breather. Olivia, go and clean the plates away or something.

DR. GOWER And mind your manners this time!

OLIVIA I always do!

JANICE No, Olivia. Be yourself. It's Zara, remember.

OLIVIA Oh, make your fucking mind up, you lot.

JANICE Perfect.

OLIVIA enters the dining room. ZARA is waiting patiently at the dinner table having had enough of her soup.

OLIVIA Hello missus. I'm Olivia, the cleaner. *(grabs the steak dinner plate)* Have you finished with that? *(indicating the soup)*

ZARA Yeah, it was nice, thanks.

OLIVIA *(looking into the bowl)* Can't have been that nice; you've fucking left half of it.

ZARA *(taken aback)* Oh. I'm sorry. I'm just stuffed, is all.

OLIVIA There's starving kids out there and you can't even polish off a fucking tin of soup?

ZARA Sorry. I... err...

OLIVIA lifts the bowls of soup to her mouth and slurps the remainder in. ZARA is gob-smacked.

OLIVIA Waste not, want not. So, what you doing here then?

ZARA I'm Zara. I'm on a date with Walter. Didn't he tell you?

OLIVIA Oh dear. Another pig in a poke.

ZARA What?

OLIVIA Never mind.

ZARA So what can you tell me about Walter? Do you know him well?

OLIVIA Not really. I've only worked here a few weeks.

ZARA Do you like it?

OLIVIA It's all right. Gets me out of the house. My dog, Scrap, went missing a couple of months since, so it's a good way to take my mind off it. I had a fish for a while, but that drowned. It's different with a dog though, ain't it?. You care more, don't ya. I don't know what to do with myself anymore. I loved that little fellow.

ZARA Oh, I'm sorry to hear that. I've got to be honest... I'm not really a fan of dogs, myself. I'm shit-scared of the things.

OLIVIA There must be something fucking wrong with you. Not liking dogs.

OLIVIA storms back into the living room with the plates and passes WALTER who returns to the dining room. She exits SL. WALTER has forgot his fake voice for his first few lines.

WALTER Desserts are looking good.

ZARA Your cleaner is a right fruitcake.

WALTER I know. She's great, isn't she!

ZARA I think she took offence to me not liking dogs.

WALTER Oh that's right. I forgot you didn't like dogs.

ZARA *(looking nervous)* You haven't got one, have you?

WALTER No, not anymore. Used to. Not for many years now.

ZARA OK. Cool. *(a brief awkward silence)* So tell me a bit about your bike, seeing as though I can't see it.

WALTER Oh right. *(coughing and forcing his "bad boy" voice back on)* The bike. *(gulp)* What do you want to know?

ZARA Well, what sort of bike is it? I've got a Honda superbike.

WALTER I've got a Honda super-duper-bike.

ZARA *(chuckles)* I've not heard of that one. How many cylinders?

WALTER *(gulp)* Erm... cylinders. Like, twelve?

ZARA They usually only make them twin or four. What engine size would that be?

WALTER Like… Four thousand cc.

ZARA Blimey. Must be fast.

WALTER Oh it is. It's like lightening down at Silverstone.

ZARA You've rode your bike round Silverstone?

WALTER Yeah. Raced round it with Valentino Rossi. He invites me there at weekends when it's quiet.

ZARA Wouldn't that be when it's busiest?

WALTER *(panicking)* I mean during the off-season. It's honestly amazing. Me, Valentino Rossi, Barry Sheene…

ZARA Well he's dead.

WALTER Erm, sorry. Not Barry Sheene. I meant Carl Fogarty.

ZARA *(sarcastic)* Understandable mistake.

WALTER Yeah. I love getting away at weekends and tearing up Silverstone. Got my lap time to just under a minute.

ZARA Jesus. That must be a world record.

WALTER Oh… Er… It is. But the guys asked me not to submit it. Makes the rest of em look bad.

ZARA Walter…

WALTER Yeah?

ZARA Why are you bullshitting me? If you're wanting to get rid of me, you could just ask me to leave.

WALTER Why do you think that?

ZARA Well, you've just been a bit of a dickhead since I got here.

WALTER That's just me. I'm just a <u>bad guy</u> I suppose.

ZARA It's just as well.

WALTER What do you mean?

ZARA I've had so many relationships with arseholes that seem nice at first. Then before you know it, boom, they sleep with your best friend, or they steal your money, or they sleep with your mother, or they get addicted to drugs, or they sleep with your brother…*(noticing WALTER's reaction)* yeah… it's happened.

WALTER So why do you like bad guys so much then?

ZARA I don't know. Most guys pretend to be nice until they've got you, then they turn into wankers. With a bad guy, you know where you stand with them from the get-go. I mean. Only an idiot would pretend to be bad, when they're actually nice, right?

WALTER *(nervously)* Yeah. Only an idiot.

Blackout.

Act 1 Scene 4 - The Dining Room Fiasco

*A week has passed. The lights return on the living room. **DEREK** is on the sofa again, this time with **JANICE**. They are both watching television. **WALTER** is pacing up and down the room looking for something. He is wearing his wife-beater vest again.*

JANICE So how are things going with Zara?

WALTER Not bad actually. We've messaged quite a lot. She seems like a lot of fun. Plus, it's funny that I can say literally anything, without offending her.

DEREK She's like the ideal woman.

JANICE *(smacking him)* Hey! You've already got the ideal woman.

WALTER *(still searching)* Where is it? Where is it? I've looked everywhere for it now.

JANICE What are you looking for?

WALTER That... *(clicking his fingers)* thing.

JANICE What thing?

WALTER You know the... err... Huh...

JANICE What's wrong?

WALTER *(looks sad)* I... I don't remember. Oh no.

DEREK It's OK, Walter. *(comically)* Just forget about it.

WALTER *(angry)* Is that supposed to be funny? *(shouting off SL)* Doctor! Doctor! Get in here.

DR. GOWER *(entering)* I don't think I've heard this one before.

WALTER It's not a joke. I forgot something. It's starting isn't it?

DR. GOWER It's OK, Walter. It will only be minor episodes for now.

WALTER I don't want any episodes. I'm supposed to be dead before any of this kicked in.

DR. GOWER Just try to relax, Walter. Come, go into the dining room. We'll talk about it at dinner.

WALTER Dinner? Won't I be eating with my date tonight?

DR. GOWER Yes. This isn't for you. I've somehow been roped into cooking for Janice and Derek, too.

DEREK Well we have been here all day!

JANICE And we really appreciate it, Doctor.

DR. GOWER Well, I thought I may as well cook for myself and Olivia whilst I was at it. Go all out.

WALTER Good man.

DR. GOWER I'll go and check on it. Go get sat down.

DR. GOWER exits SL. WALTER, JANICE and DEREK move to the dining room. The lights flip over. There are now four chairs at the dinner table.JANICE and DEREK take a seat.

DEREK I'm looking forward to this. I haven't had a decent home cooked meal in months.

JANICE *(giving him a backhand)* You cheeky sod. I cooked for you the other day.

DEREK I said <u>decent</u>!

JANICE gives him another smack. OLIVIA enters SR holding a dishcloth. She places it on the dinner table.

OLIVIA There you are, Walter. I've just had to clean the toilet. It was a right mess. *(to JANICE)* Weren't you the last one in there?

JANICE All right, Olivia *(stressing discretion)*. I've had a dicky tummy the last couple of days. No need to tell everyone.

OLIVIA And another thing, I've only just given the hallway the once over, and someone's trod in cat shit on the way in.

WALTER Don't worry. That can wait. Doctor Gower has made you some dinner.

OLIVIA That's nice of him, but I need to find the culprit first. Can't have 'em traipsing it all though the house, can we? Feet up everybody!

Everyone lifts their feet up and OLIVIA sets about checking the soles of all their shoes. DR. GOWER enters the dining room from the living room.

DR. GOWER Olivia! You haven't washed the dishes from lunch! Dinner is almost ready, and we don't have enough plates for everyone.

OLIVIA *(still checking shoes)* I've been a mite busy, Doctor. You'll have to clean them yourself. Sorry.

DR. GOWER Well, I would have done, but the dishcloth isn't in there. *(spotting it on the table)* Oh! Here it is. What's it doing here? I wish you'd leave things where they belong, Olivia. Oh well, what's one more job to add to my repertoire. *(storms off SL)*

OLIVIA *(arriving at DEREK's shoes)* Here's the culprit. I might have known. Still not changed your clothes either I see. I recognise that stain. *(pointing at a mark on his shirt)* Right, off it comes. *(slides his shoe off)* Have you got a wire brush, Walter?

WALTER Not that I know of.

DEREK It's OK. Just put them outside the front door. I'll sort them out myself when I get home.

OLIVIA *(ignoring him)* It's OK. I'll find something. *(exits SR with the shoe)*

JANICE So, who's the date tonight with?

WALTER Fran.

JANICE I think I prefer the other one.

DEREK I don't think either are suited to him.

JANICE You would say that.

WALTER Donald's right.

DEREK Derek.

WALTER I made up a character for both of them. Who's to say if they'd like the real me?

DR. GOWER enters the dining room from the living room with place settings enough for four and sets the table.

JANICE Thanks again for this, Doctor.

WALTER *(spotting a photo frame amongst his fake certificates and trophies)* Is that a picture of me and my old dog, Buster? Where did that come from?

Everyone turns to look.

DR. GOWER Oh yes! I found it in one of the drawers in the desk I work at upstairs. I thought it would be a nice photo to have up.

OLIVIA *(enters SR)* It's no good. It's really caked in there.

No one notices her and carry on with the conversation.

WALTER Well. It needs to come down. Fran is terrified of dogs.

OLIVIA grabs the fork from DEREK's place setting and begins scraping off the dog mess from the base of his shoe.

JANICE No. You're thinking of Zara. Fran is scared of ghosts or something.

WALTER Oh that's right!

OLIVIA places the fork back where she got it from. The others turn back towards the front.

DEREK It's only a photo, anyway. I doubt she's scared of <u>pictures</u> of dogs.
OLIVIA *(to DEREK)* Right, young man. Here's your shoe.
DEREK I told you, you didn't have to, but... Thanks.
OLIVIA It's no bother. It'd have been on my mind all evening.
DR. GOWER Come on, Olivia. You can help me serve dinner.
OLIVIA All right.

DR. GOWER and OLIVIA exit SL.

JANICE It's really nice of your doctor to do all this for us.
WALTER Yeah. He's a good man. To be honest, and don't let him know I told you this; He's probably the best friend I've got. I like winding him up, but... I don't think I could have gone through all this without him.

DR. GOWER and OLIVIA return with the food. JANICE and DEREK take their seats.

JANICE *(as it's being plated up)* This looks fantastic, doctor!
DEREK Aye! Much better than the slop I get at home!
JANICE *(hitting him)* Oy!
DR. GOWER It's nothing special.
JANICE I'm just glad I'm feeling up to food again.
OLIVIA I'm not surprised after you'd pebble dashed the water closet.
JANICE Olivia!
OLIVIA And the stench! Oooooh fuck me! There was a dense smog in the air. And the window was open at that. It was so thick my eyes were streaming. Even the extractor fan was struggling.
JANICE *(begging)* Please stop.
OLIVIA Anyone that leaves a deposit like that definitely needs to seek medical attention. I think you need the good doctor here to give you a rectal exam cause I fear something's crawled up your arse and died.
JANICE *(mortified)* Kill me now.

DR. GOWER and OLIVIA finish serving the food, place the serving dishes to one side and join the others at the table.

WALTER Ooh. Here's one. Doctor, doctor! I've got a bladder infection.

DR. GOWER Sounds like urine trouble. Can I request we please stop talking about the toilet right before dinner?

JANICE Agreed!

DR. GOWER OK everyone. Enjoy!

*They all tuck in. **WALTER** is a bit fidgety whilst they all eat. **DEREK** furrows his brows on his first mouthful.*

DEREK Erm... Doctor? What's in this?

DR. GOWER It's my speciality.

DEREK It tastes like shit!

DR. GOWER You ungrateful sod.

JANICE I think it's lovely.

OLIVIA Get it down ya.

***DEREK** continues to eat. It tastes OK now.*

JANICE *(noticing **WALTER**)* What's the matter, Walter? You're not nervous are you?

WALTER No. I mean. It is the second date. I wouldn't know what to talk about, even if I was being myself.

DR. GOWER Have you considered the potential implications of what you could be putting these girls through?

WALTER What do you mean?

DR. GOWER Well, let's say one of these girls falls for you. Then what?

WALTER Then lucky her. She inherits some of my money.

DR. GOWER It's always about the money with you, isn't it, Walter. Don't you remember a time when you didn't have wealth? When you couldn't buy whatever you wanted on a whim? What was on your mind back then? What did you think about? Can you even remember?

WALTER Yes! I remember thinking, "Oh man, I hope I'm rich one day!".

DR. GOWER Of course. *(rolls his eyes)* But not everyone is like you, Walter. These girls may actually care more about you than your money. Did you ever think about that?

WALTER So?

DR. GOWER So? So, what happens when they find out you'll be dead soon? Do you really think it's fair to play with these girls' emotions, only to put them through the heartbreak of your death should one of them fall in love with you?

WALTER *(thinking hard on that for a moment)* Oh for God's sake, Doctor. Way to kill the mood. Look, don't worry. I promise it'll be fine.

OLIVIA *(spotting the photo of the dog)* Oh, I didn't know you had a dog, Mr. Emerson.

WALTER I haven't. Not anymore.

OLIVIA Oh, I know the feeling. The day my dog, Scrap, ran off, I was ever so upset. *(tears form)* I would call him and call him, and he never came home. *(vacantly)* Scrap! *(to the group)* I called. *(back to being vacant)* Scrap! *(pause)* Scrap! *(pause)* Scrap!

DEREK I've got an old bike in my garage if you want that?

JANICE Be nice!

*As she says this, **JANICE** gives **DEREK** a nudge with her elbow, who drops a dollop of food from his fork onto the floor.*

JANICE Ooops! Sorry.

OLIVIA It's all right. I'll get it. *(checks her pockets, then looks on the table)* Has anyone seen the dishcloth? I'm sure I left it here on the table. I can't go about woman's work without it.

DR. GOWER I left it in the kitchen after I did the dishes, where it belongs!

OLIVIA Oh you didn't do the dishes with it, did ya?

DR. GOWER Yes, why? What's the problem? What was it doing in here anyway?

OLIVIA Well, I ran out of J-Cloths, so I used the dishcloth for the toilet!

Everyone drops their knives and forks upon hearing this and spits their current mouthful of food back onto the plate.

DR. GOWER *(in a rage)* What? That's disgusting!

OLIVIA *(explaining)* I was just giving it the once over.

DR. GOWER You can't clean the toilet with the same cloth we use for the dishes!

OLIVIA I know, but thanks to her *(pointing at **JANICE**)* it was heavily soiled. I took a look and there was tractor treads all round the pan.

JANICE *(immense embarrassment)* Olivia, please!

OLIVIA *(ignoring her)* Well, I couldn't leave it like that could I?

JANICE Olivia, I'm a lady. I don't want you discussing my trip to the toilet.

OLIVIA I don't know about lady, I thought I was cleaning up after a combine harvester. Post tatie picking! *(JANICE buries her head in her hand)*

DR. GOWER *(still fuming)* You've ruined everyone's dinner! Do you have any idea how unhygienic this is?

OLIVIA Don't talk so wet. It's good for the immune system.

DR. GOWER Someone could get typhoid from this.

OLIVIA Oh what a load of cobblers. They be all right. Whatever doesn't kill em only makes em stronger.

DR. GOWER I think I'm going to be sick. Take everyone's plates away.

OLIVIA *(standing)* Blimey! I think you're overreacting a tad.

OLIVIA grabs everyone's plates and exits SL.

JANICE I can't believe I ate that.

DEREK At least it was your shit. How do you feel for the rest of us? *(to the others)* I told you I could taste shit from that first forkful.

WALTER I'm glad I didn't have any. Wouldn't want shit breath before my date. *(laughs as he checks his watch)* Speaking of which, she'll be here any minute! It's probably a good thing that dinner was cut short.

DEREK Which one did you say was coming over?

WALTER Zara.

JANICE I thought you said it was Fran tonight.

WALTER It is.

JANICE But you just said Zara.

WALTER Did I?

JANICE Yes.

WALTER I'm sure it's… erm... *(laughs to himself)* I can't remember who's coming. Two seconds. I'll check my messages.

WALTER takes his phone out to check his messages. After a brief pause, he looks up, shocked.

JANICE What's wrong?

WALTER I've arranged for them both to come, tonight. *(the doorbell rings)* Oh fu--------

Blackout.

End of Act I

Act 2 Scene 1 - The Farce

Act II begins where Act I left off. There are now only two chairs at the dining table.

WALTER Oh my God! What am I going to do? One of them are here already.

DEREK *(praying)* Please tell me this really happening. Please don't let this be a dream.

DR. GOWER Maybe they're both out there.

DEREK That would be the best thing ever!

JANICE It's OK. We can work around this.

WALTER Work around it? I can barely keep up one act, never mind two at once.

JANICE We'll just take the laptop into the kitchen, out of the way, and you can keep one of the girls in here, and the other one in the living room.

*The doorbell rings again. **WALTER** screams.*

DR. GOWER You'd better get that.

WALTER I can't go! I don't which one it is. If it's Fran, she can't see me dressed like this. *(to **DR. GOWER**)* You'll have to answer the door and tell me who it is.

DR. GOWER *(sigh)* Fine! *(exits SR)*

WALTER Into the living room. Quick!

The three of them run into the living room. The lights flip over.

JANICE This is do-able. You can wear your suit over the top of your vest, then you can easily whip it off, as and when.

WALTER Good idea. You two need to clear out of here, fast.

***JANICE** grabs the laptop and **DEREK** and they rush off SL.
DR. GOWER enters SR and comes into the living room, leaving **FRAN** in the dining room.*

DR. GOWER It's Miss Phillips. She's waiting in the dining room.

WALTER Good. OK, get in the kitchen with the others. You'll need to make some extra food. *(**DR. GOWER** starts to leave)* Doctor, doctor. A, E, I, O, U.

DR. GOWER Sounds like you've got a case of irritable vowel syndrome. Is this really the time for that?

DR. GOWER exits. WALTER stamps in frustration. He grabs his motorbike helmet and leathers and puts them on, along with the wig. He enters the dining room and the lights come up in there. FRAN is standing in the room with her back to WALTER. She is wearing a light-coloured dress.

WALTER Hello again, you sexy little minx. *(slaps her on the bottom)*
FRAN *(turning around)* What in the name of…
WALTER Uh-oh!

WALTER runs back into the corridor between the rooms. He removes his helmet and leathers in the corridor and enters the living room. He throws his wig towards the back end of SL and grabs his suit which was over the back of the sofa before putting it on. He dashes back into the dining room, out of breath.

WALTER *(as if nothing has happened)* Oh, hello, Fran, darling. Are you well?
FRAN Well I was. There was someone in here a moment ago and he… he…
WALTER He what, Fran, dear?
FRAN He slapped my posterior!
WALTER *(over the top shock)* NO!
FRAN Yes! Who on earth was it? I couldn't see their face. They were wearing a helmet.
WALTER *(pretending to think)* Helmet… helmet... Ah! Of course! It must have been the butler. Wilson.
FRAN Wilson? But the man that answered the door was the chef from the other night. Alejandro wasn't it?
WALTER Yes, exactly. See what I mean. He's mad. One minute he's a chef, the next he's a butler, next he's harassing vulnerable women. I will ensure that I have a stern word with him.
FRAN I should hope so. Carrying on like that. The man should be ashamed of himself.
WALTER Here, allow me to take your coat. *(removes her coat and hangs it on the coat stand)*
FRAN Thank you, Walter. *(spotting the shelf)* Oh. You have some different awards.
WALTER *(panicking)* No I don't.

FRAN *(picking one up)* 'World's Baddest Guy 2008' *(WALTER snatches it from her)* There's an award for that? What on earth did you do, Walter?

WALTER *(he shoves the rest of his fake props into a nearby box)* Ha-ha, these are just 'joke' trophies. Alejandro must have put them out for a laugh.

FRAN What a strange man.

The doorbell rings.

WALTER Oh sh… sh… sugar delivery man is here.

FRAN Sugar delivery man? Is that even a thing?

WALTER It is if you're living a complicated life. Why don't I show you into the living room?

FRAN But, shouldn't you get the door?

WALTER No need. The doc will get it.

FRAN Doc?

WALTER The butler… Wilson… Alejandro… Whatever his name is. You just come with me, sweetness.

WALTER links arms with FRAN and escorts her to the living room. DR. GOWER enters SL.

WALTER Well, I'd better get the door.

FRAN *(turns to him)* Isn't that what <u>he's</u> here for? *(turning to DR. GOWER)*

WALTER No, no. I'll get this one. I don't like to overwork him.

DR. GOWER *(sarcastically)* HA!

FRAN turns her back on DR. GOWER. DR. GOWER is trying to get WALTER's attention whilst she's not looking. He is pointing at his own head.

WALTER *(trying to work out what's being said)* I, guess, I'd, better… err… <u>head</u> in there and get the door?

DR. GOWER shakes his head violently. FRAN quickly turns around to look at him. He quickly smiles as though nothing is wrong. She turns back to WALTER. DR. GOWER is miming 'opening a door' and then pointing at his own head again.

WALTER *(still trying to guess)* Door? Opening? Doctor? Forehead?

*FRAN turns to look at **DR. GOWER** again, just missing his actions. She turns back.*

FRAN What is going on?
WALTER Nothing. I'm just saying. I need to answer the door.

DR. GOWER now pretends to be smoking and pointing at his own head.

FRAN Then shouldn't you be going?
WALTER *(trying to figure out again)* I am. I just first need to… err… smoke? Smoking? Cig?

DR. GOWER nods frantically at this. He then starts to do a big letter 'W' with his arms.

WALTER Cig! Right cig! Got it!
FRAN Cig? Oh you don't partake in them, do you? You could be dead in years, if you smoke those things.
WALTER Oh, in that case I should probably take it up.
FRAN I'm sorry?
WALTER No I just… When I says cig, I mean… *(resumes guessing)* W… Cig… W…? Wig? *(realising)* Wig! Of course! Wig!
FRAN Wig?

*Confused, **FRAN** looks towards **DR. GOWER**. Whilst her back is turned, **WALTER** points towards the wig in the corner of the room by **DR. GOWER**. **FRAN** turns back to **WALTER**. **DR. GOWER** retrieves the wig whilst she isn't looking. He looks at **WALTER** and mouths the words 'now what?' and shrugs.*

WALTER Wig. Yes. What I mean is… Er…
DR. GOWER Miss Phillips?

*As she turns her head, **DR. GOWER** throws the wig over the top of her. **WALTER** catches it and hides it behind his back.*

FRAN Yes?
DR. GOWER Why don't you have a seat whilst you're waiting?
WALTER I'll just go and get the door. *(escapes into the dining room)*

FRAN Well I suppose my behind is safer on the sofa whilst <u>you're</u> around.

DR. GOWER Whatever do you mean?

FRAN You know perfectly well what I mean, Alejandro.

DR. GOWER Alejandro?

FRAN Yes. You should be ashamed of yourself, you perverse man.

DR. GOWER Perverse? I haven't done anything.

*The lights go down on the living room. **WALTER** takes his suit off exposing his wife-beater vest. He pulls his wig on and runs off SR. He returns followed by **ZARA** who is carrying her handbag.*

ZARA *(shivering)* It's cold out. I'm glad I brought a coat. You were even longer answering the door today.

WALTER *(posh voice by mistake)* Sorry about that. Allow me to take your coat, madam.

ZARA Oh, what a gentleman. Who says chivalry's dead?

WALTER *(realising)* Oh crap, you're right. *(throws her coat on the floor)* Hang it up yourself, you lazy cow.

*Gobsmacked, **ZARA** picks up her coat from the floor. She goes to hang it up, but notices **FRAN**'s coat already on the stand.*

ZARA Oh. Have you got company?

WALTER *(spotting the coat and panicking)* No… err… that's Olivia's.

ZARA Oh, the cleaner. Is she here every day?

WALTER Most days. I'm a very messy man.

ZARA You just need a good woman in your life. *(hangs her coat up)* So, what's the plan tonight? Still can't leave the house?

WALTER No, not yet, I'm afraid. Doctor's orders.

ZARA That's a shame. So, have you got any films we could watch?

WALTER Yes, I've got some.

ZARA Can I see what you've got?

WALTER Yes. The TV's just through here. *(walking towards the living room followed by **ZARA**)* Wait! *(stopping and spinning around)*

ZARA *(startled)* What's wrong?

WALTER It… err… Might be a mess in there. Let me just quickly look around. You wait here.

***WALTER** sneaks into the living room. The lights flip over. Remaining out of sight of **FRAN**, who has her back to the door, he quickly puts his*

*suit back on and dumps the wig behind the sofa out of sight. **FRAN** and
DR. GOWER are in the middle of their argument from earlier.*

DR. GOWER *(whilst **WALTER** is changing)* I don't know how many
times I have to tell you… It wasn't me!

FRAN Are you denying placing your hand on my bottom?

DR. GOWER I am <u>absolutely</u> denying it. I don't know how you dare
accuse me of such a thing.

FRAN *(spotting **WALTER**, just missing his quick change)* Ah, Walter.
Alejandro here, denies any wrongdoing with regards to my backside.

DR. GOWER Why is she calling me that? Is this because it was what
you called me as a joke on your first date?

FRAN A joke? You'd better not be playing games with me, Walter.

WALTER Of course not, Fran darling. It was Wilson the butler that
sexually assaulted you.

FRAN But you said Wilson the butler was Alejandro the chef?

WALTER That's right.

FRAN *(pointing to **DR. GOWER**)* But <u>that's</u> Alejandro the chef.

DR. GOWER No. I'm Doctor Gower, the doctor.

FRAN The doctor?

WALTER Don't confuse him, Fran. He's a very disturbed schizophrenic.

DR. GOWER A schizophrenic? I am not.

WALTER Yes you are, Doctor. *(to **FRAN**)* He isn't aware of the
condition himself. He can dip in and out of all sorts of different
characters at random.

DR. GOWER *(angrily to **WALTER**)* I'm going to kill you.

WALTER There's Morris the Murderer.

FRAN The murderer? Good heavens.

ZARA *(from the dining room)* Walter?

WALTER *(hearing **ZARA**)* Err… *(to **FRAN**)* Yes, the murderer. Quick!
I'd better hide you in the cupboard before he gets out of control.

DR. GOWER *(shouting)* Out of control?

WALTER Oh God! It's starting. Quick! *(dragging her over to the
cupboard and bundling her inside)*

FRAN But I don't want to go in the…

***WALTER** slams the cupboard door on **FRAN** and throws his suit
jacket onto the floor just as **ZARA** enters the living room. **FRAN** is
repeatedly banging on the door whilst **WALTER** stands in front of it
holding it shut.*

ZARA You've had long enough to check if it's a mess or not. What was all the noise? I thought I heard shouting.

WALTER Yes. That was Doctor Gower here.

ZARA Isn't he Antwon the gardener?

DR. GOWER No! I'm Doctor Gower the doctor!

WALTER That's right! Antwon's twin brother!

ZARA And both twins work for you? Doesn't that get confusing?

WALTER You have no idea.

ZARA *(noticing **WALTER**'s normal hair)* Walter! What's happened to your hair?

WALTER *(touching his head and panicking)* Oh, err, Doctor Gower, cut a great big chunk out of it by mistake. I had to have him cut the whole thing.

ZARA In the time since I last saw you?

WALTER Yes, he's a very fast, but very clumsy worker.

DR. GOWER *(trying to help with the lie)* They call me butterfingers at the hospital.

ZARA I hope you never have to operate on me. *(spotting the suit on the floor)* You didn't do a very good job of tidying up, did you. *(bundling up the suit in her arms)*

WALTER It's OK, just leave it there. I'll sort it later.

ZARA I'm only picking it up off the floor. *(spotting cupboard door banging)* Is there someone trapped in there?

WALTER Err... Not someone. Something!

ZARA Like what?

WALTER It's a… a… *(to himself)* Come on Walter, think. What was it? *(gives up)* Just give me a second.

*WALTER indicates to **DR. GOWER** for him to swap places with him. They do and **WALTER** exits SL. **DR. GOWER** and **ZARA** share an awkward smile as he holds the cupboard door shut. **WALTER** returns reading a piece of paper. **ZARA** catches a glimpse of what he's holding.*

ZARA Is that my profile page?

WALTER *(scanning the page)* I was just making sure that… *(finding the information by tracing the page with his finger)* Dog! *(tossing the paper aside)* That's it I remember now, big dog in there. *(pointing at the cupboard)*

ZARA *(petrified)* What? In the cupboard?

WALTER *(ushering her off SL)* You go wait in the kitchen whilst I get rid of it.

ZARA, still holding the suit, runs off SL.

WALTER Wait. No! I need the suit! Doctor, quick go and get it.

DR. GOWER heads towards SL, but as he leaves the cupboard door, FRAN pushes it open slightly.

WALTER No! *(he races to the cupboard door and shuts FRAN back in)*
DR. GOWER Ooops. Sorry.
DEREK *(off SL)* Shit! One of em's coming in here!
JANICE *(off SL)* Quick! Out the back door!
ZARA *(off SL)* Who's there?

The sound of the back door opening and slamming shut is heard. WALTER and DR. GOWER share panicked looks as they hear the commotion off SL.

FRAN Walter! I demand you let me out this second.
WALTER Quick, Doctor. There's no time. Give me your suit.
DR. GOWER I'll do no such thing.
WALTER Fran can't see me like this.
DR. GOWER I don't care.
WALTER Give it to me, Doctor.
DR. GOWER No!
WALTER Give it to me!
DR. GOWER No.
WALTER Right!

WALTER lunges at DR. GOWER and tackles him to the floor behind the sofa, out of sight. Screaming is heard. DR. GOWER's clothing comes flying into view over the top of the sofa. WALTER stands, holding DR. GOWER's suit bunched up in his arms. DR. GOWER stands up in his underwear.

DR. GOWER *(grabbing the suit)* Give it back!
WALTER *(still holding one end of the suit)* It's for my health!
DR. GOWER *(pulling at it)* Sod your bleeding health!

They cease their game of tug-of-war when WALTER realises they've left the cupboard unguarded.

WALTER *(realising)* Uh-oh. The cupboard!

*They both look at the cupboard as the door begins to open. **WALTER**
pushes **DR. GOWER** over the sofa in front of it and out of view of
FRAN who comes wandering out of the cupboard.*

FRAN What on earth was that about? Did I hear you refer to me as a dog?
WALTER No, no. I was just dealing with Malcolm the Murderer.
FRAN I thought it was Morris the Murderer.
WALTER Err… it is. *(realising his mistake)* But he changed
   personalities again.
FRAN You mean to say he has <u>two</u> homicidal personalities?
WALTER Yes, but one isn't quite as bad the other. One of them doesn't
   harm women and children.
FRAN Are we safe now?
WALTER Yes. I've given him his medicine.
FRAN Oh good. My friends would be awfully worried if I told them I
   was here with a murderer.
DR. GOWER *(standing to be seen)* I AM NOT A MURDERER!
FRAN *(seeing the part-naked doctor)* What in the world?
WALTER I find it best to ignore him when he's being Nigel the nudist.
DR. GOWER *(shouting in anger)* Nigel the…
WALTER Yes Nigel. Please go into the kitchen and check on our <u>other</u>
   problem.
DR. GOWER *(defeated)* Yes, sir. *(exits SL)*
FRAN That man gets stranger by the second. *(looking at his vest)*
   Whatever are you wearing? What happened to your suit?
WALTER The dog ragged it off whilst I was wrestling with it. *(holding
   the suit up)* It's no good now you see. It's all creased.
FRAN Dog? What dog?
WALTER *(realising)* The… err… dog personality that Doctor Gower
   sometimes takes on. Larry the labrador. He's not been house-trained
   yet.
FRAN You mean to say that Doctor Gower also takes on the personality
   of a canine?
WALTER That's right.
FRAN How bizarre. *(spotting the profile print out)* Is that a printout of
   another girl's profile page?
WALTER Nope! *(quickly grabs it, screws it up and tosses it away)*
FRAN Walter! Is one girl not enough for you?

WALTER Believe me, it's more than enough. *(quickly changing the subject)* Erm... maybe we should head back into the dining room. Dinner will likely be ready soon. *(he places the suit on the sofa)*

FRAN Smashing! I'm a bit famished after all this excitement.

*On the way out, **FRAN** spots the wig behind sofa. She picks it up and holds it out at arms-length.*

FRAN What's something like this doing in here?

WALTER That's one of Harold the hairdresser's practice wigs.

FRAN Oh come on! How many different personalities does that man have?

WALTER *(aside)* As many as I need to get through the evening. *(to FRAN)* I wouldn't handle that if I were you. He's been practising lice removal on that one.

FRAN *(dropping it back where she found it)* How ghastly.

WALTER Come along now.

__WALTER__ places the bunched-up suit on the sofa and they both exit into the dining room, which has the lights down. __DR. GOWER__ re-enters with a cowering __ZARA__ behind him.

ZARA Are you sure it's gone?

DR. GOWER Yes, I heard them leave.

ZARA And you say it ripped your suit off?

DR. GOWER Oh yes. Vicious little mutt. You were right to flee. *(spotting his suit)* Oh look. A spare one. That's handy. *(starts to re-dress himself)*

ZARA When I first ran into the kitchen, I saw a man and a woman run out of the back door. Who were they?

DR. GOWER Oh them? Erm... just the kitchen staff.

ZARA Then why did they run?

DR. GOWER They're very shy. They don't like to be seen.

ZARA Oh. Are you eating with us tonight, Doctor?

DR. GOWER No. I've already eaten.

ZARA Anything nice?

DR. GOWER It was a plate of shit to be honest.

ZARA What?

DR. GOWER Don't worry. Yours will be much nicer.

ZARA Maybe the cleaner, then? There was a lot of food cooking in there for just me and Walter.

DR. GOWER Walter has a big appetite.

ZARA At least I'll be getting some meat tonight.

DR. GOWER *(shocked)* I beg your pardon?

ZARA The steak in the kitchen.

DR. GOWER Oh yes, the food. Of course. It will be ready soon. I shall go and get it.

ZARA OK. I'll wait in the dining room. *(she heads towards it)*

DR.GOWER OK... *(just as **ZARA** is about to enter the dining room)* NO! Ha-ha. Walter said the two of you would be eating on trays in front of the TV tonight. So that... erm... you can watch a movie.

ZARA Awesome. That's my kind of night. *(sitting on the sofa and putting her handbag down)*

> **DR. GOWER** *exits SL. The lights flip.* **WALTER** *and* **FRAN** *are sitting at the dining room table.*

FRAN *(messaging on her phone)* They really are concerned, bless them. I'm sorry that I'm always using my mobile phone.

WALTER Don't be. I completely understand.

FRAN I've been looking forward to this meal all day. There aren't many people that can cook up a decent vegan dish, you know.

WALTER I do have one hell of a chef slash doctor slash butler slash tailor.

> **JANICE** *and* **DEREK** *enter SR.*

JANICE *(whispering to **DEREK**)* I'm telling you; I think that Zara saw us run out the back.

> **JANICE** *spots* **FRAN** *and panics.* **WALTER** *spots them and gives them a panicked look.* **DEREK** *and* **JANICE** *stumble in the panic, knocking the coat stand over. They split up and run in opposite directions;* **DEREK** *dashes back off SR and* **JANICE** *runs into the small corridor that connects the two rooms.* **FRAN** *spins around at the sound of the commotion. Lights come up in the living room.* **ZARA** *is sat looking bored on the sofa. Throughout the following scene* **JANICE**'s *head appears in the doorway of both rooms a couple of times each as she tries to plan her escape.*

FRAN What was that?

WALTER What was what?

FRAN Something just knocked over the coat stand.

WALTER Oh it was… err… probably the ghost.

FRAN Ghost? Oh, please tell me that you're joking. I'm terribly afraid of the supernatural.

WALTER *(annoyed at himself for forgetting this detail)* Of course you are. It was the <u>wind</u> then.

FRAN I'm being serious. I know it's embarrassing, but that sort of thing really scares me. Promise me that it's not haunted here!

WALTER Well, I've lived here for six hundred years and never noticed anything.

FRAN *(chuckling slightly)* That's not funny, Walter.

WALTER I do think my cleaner may be a ghost, though.

FRAN Really? What makes you say that?

WALTER I've had my suspicions since she walked through door.

(FRAN gives him a sarcastic look)

The lights go down in the dining room. JANICE decides to creep through the living room. She sneaks behind the sofa, but slips on the wig which comes flying out into view. JANICE crashes to the ground causing ZARA to jump up.

ZARA Oh my God! Are you OK? *(going round to help her up)*

JANICE Yeah, I just slipped.

ZARA I recognise you. Aren't you one of the kitchen staff I saw running out the back?

JANICE Erm… Am I?

ZARA That's what I was told.

JANICE Then yes… *(unconvincingly)* Yes I am. I'm Janice. Nice to meet you.

OLIVIA *(entering SL)* What's all the banging about? *(also slips on the wig and crashes to the floor)*

ZARA *(helping up OLIVIA as well)* Bloody hell! Are <u>you</u> all right? *(picks up the wig)* What is this thing anyway.

JANICE *(snatching it from her hands)* This is… erm. Olivia's duster.

ZARA *(snatching it back)* It doesn't look like a duster.

OLIVIA *(snatching it)* Get your fucking hands off it. Cleaning's <u>my</u> job. *(starts dusting with it)*

ZARA *(snatching it back and taking a closer look)* It looks like a wig.

JANICE *(panicking and snatching it again)* Oh yeah. That's right. It's…err… mine! *(puts it on)*

ZARA Really? Why are you carrying it round with you?

JANICE Sometimes I just fancy a change.

ZARA *(snatching it off her head)* You lot must think I'm thick as pig shit. Is this what Walter's been wearing?

JANICE *(trying to snatch it back creating a tug-of-war situation)* No it really is mine.

ZARA *(pulling it back towards her)* I don't believe you.

JANICE *(pulling it back towards her)* Well it's true.

OLIVIA Knock it off, you two.

ZARA *(pulling)* Give it here.

JANICE *(pulling)* It's mine.

ZARA *(pulling)* It's not.

On this final pull, the pair knock the urn and it wobbles. JANICE releases the wig to catch the urn. ZARA moves downstage, in front of the sofa, to properly inspect the wig. The lights in the dining room come up briefly.

WALTER I shall just go and check on our dinner, darling.

FRAN Very well.

WALTER leaves the dining room into the corridor between the two rooms. The lights go down in the dining room.

ZARA This is definitely Walter's wig, the lying little git.

JANICE *(moving over to her)* I can explain.

OLIVIA *(moving over to them and standing between them)* Put that urn back, missus. His Lordship gave me strict instructions not to touch it again after I nearly turned him into a shake n' vac the other day. I'll be in line at the job centre in the flick of a duster if anything happens to it.

ZARA Why? Who's in there?

JANICE Walter's dad.

ZARA Oh shit. Quick, put it back, then. I don't want him kicking me out... Not before I've had some grub at least.

WALTER enters the living room and the three ladies spin around turning their back on the audience. JANICE has the urn upright behind her back. She is trying to pass it on to OLIVIA who is reluctant to take it.

WALTER Erm... What's going on?

ALL Nothing...

WALTER *(to JANICE)* What are you doing in here?

JANICE shoves the urn into OLIVIA's hands, who takes it horizontally.
OLIVIA now tries to shove it into ZARA's hands, who also refuses to
take it. JANICE walks over to WALTER as she answers him.

JANICE I was just… err… checking how Zara liked her steak.

WALTER Why you?

JANICE As you know I'm one of the kitchen staff.

WALTER Kitchen staff? *(playing along, assuming she's saying it to*
help him out) Oh. Err… Right. Yes. My employee. I'm just about to
check on dinner. Could you come help me?

JANICE I'll be through in a minute. *(trying to usher him off SL)* No need
to wait for me.

WALTER *(to OLIVIA, stopping before JANICE gets him completely*
out) What are you up to?

OLIVIA Me? Erm, no, nothing. I'm not doing anything wrong.

OLIVIA shoves it into ZARA's hands who takes it vertically, but upside
down causing the ashes to pour onto the floor.

WALTER Hmm. *(to ZARA)* Are you OK? *(she gives him an*
acknowledging nod) OK then. I won't be long. *(exits SL)*

ZARA and OLIVIA turn back to the audience simultaneously. JANICE
heads back to join them.

ZARA That was a close one.

OLIVIA I thought we'd fucked it.

JANICE Quick! Return it before he comes ba… *(noticing the upside-*
down urn) No!

ZARA Oh bollocks.

OLIVIA What the fuck have you done?

ZARA Me? You must have passed it to me like that?

OLIVIA Well she *(indicating JANICE)* shouldn't have picked it up in
the place.

JANICE I stopped it from smashing because she *(indicating ZARA)*
nearly knocked it off.

ZARA *(holding up the wig)* I was just trying to prove that Walter had
been wearing a wig.

JANICE *(snatching the wig and launching it off SL)* Forget about the bloody wig for one second will you. We need to sort this out, or Walter will never speak to any of us again.

OLIVIA *(indicating the mound of ashes)* And I've just fucking cleaned up in here this afternoon. Now look at it. *(marches off SL)*

JANICE Hurry. *(starts searching the room)* We have to find something to get it back into the urn.

ZARA *(putting the empty urn on the sofa and helping to search)* Like what?

JANICE *(stressing urgency)* I don't know! A dustpan and brush or something! Anything! Just hurry.

Their search leads them meeting face to face at the back of the stage. Suddenly the sound of a vacuum cleaner being turned on is heard. The pair look up at each other in horror before turning to face the front, just as OLIVIA enters SL with the vacuum cleaner and rolls it over the ashes.

OLIVIA There! Good as new! *(victoriously rubbing her hands together)*

JANICE *(pure dread)* Olivia! What have you done?

OLIVIA Cleaned up the mess.

ZARA That was Walter's dad's ashes you've just sucked up.

OLIVIA *(genuinely only just realising)* Oh yeah. No matter. Easily fixed.

OLIVIA removes the collecting chamber from the vacuum cleaner. She grabs the urn off the sofa and pours the contents of the vacuum cleaner chamber into the urn. JANICE puts both hands on the sides of her head in pure horror.

ZARA What are you doing?

OLIVIA This isn't my first rodeo, you know.

ZARA You can't do that.

OLIVIA Have you got a better fucking idea?

WALTER *(shouting from off stage left)* Janice!

JANICE Oh crap. He's coming. *(runs to OLIVIA)* Quick put it back. *(grabs at the container)*

OLIVIA *(pulling away)* Let go of it you silly cow. I've nearly finished now.

JANICE There's no time.

JANICE gives one final pull and a cloud of ash and dust covers the pair of them.

OLIVIA Now look what you've gone and done you daft tart.
JANICE Oh no. Walter's gonna kill us.
ZARA Quick! Get in the cupboard and clean yourselves off!

*ZARA snatches the urn from them and quickly bundles the pair, along with the vacuum cleaner, into the cupboard. She returns the urn to its shelf just as **WALTER** re-enters SL barely missing the chaos.*

WALTER Where did those two go?
ZARA *(shrugs)* No idea. *(she quickly grabs him by the arm and pulls him to the sofa to distract him)* Why don't you come and sit down with me. I've barely seen you tonight.
WALTER Erm... OK.
ZARA So what are we watching whilst we eat?
WALTER Whilst?
ZARA Yes. The doctor said that we were eating in here, on trays.
WALTER Yes, that would make sense. We can watch whatever you want, darling.
ZARA Aww. How sweet. *(gives him a peck on the cheek then picks up the remote)*
WALTER *(realising)* I mean... give me that. *(snatching the remote)* I'll decide. *(macho)* The remote is controlled by the men.
ZARA OK then. I don't mind anyway.

*WALTER is about to turn the television on, when **DR. GOWER** enters with two meals.*

DR. GOWER Which room are these ones for?
ZARA This one of course. Where else would they be going?
WALTER *(looking at them)* No, those are for next door.
ZARA Next door?
DR. GOWER He means the front door.
WALTER Do I? I mean... I do?
DR. GOWER Yes... err... the dog. You told me to put some food out for the dog.
WALTER Yes, that's right.
ZARA Why is it still out there?
WALTER It's the neighbours dog. It's always escaping. He's on his way over to collect it. I said I'd feed it whilst it was here.

ZARA That's very thoughtful of you. Just don't let it back in here. Can I nip to the loo before dinner?

WALTER Yes. It's just down the corridor to the right of the front door.

DR. GOWER First door on the left.

ZARA *(heads towards the dining room)* Thanks.

DR GOWER & WALTER No problem... *(slight pause)* NO!

WALTER rushes in front of her and blocks her path.

ZARA What's the matter?

WALTER I err... I don't know I can't think of anything. *(looks to DR. GOWER for help)*

DR. GOWER *(improvising)* The dog is still in the dining room.

ZARA *(pure fear)* Really?

WALTER *(also to DR. GOWER)* Really?

ZARA Why?

DR. GOWER *(making it up as he goes along)* I didn't have the heart to leave it in the cold, so I chained it up in the dining room.

ZARA But I'm busting for a wee.

DR. GOWER *(pointing SL)* If you go through the kitchen and out the back door, you can walk around to the front of the house and come back in that way!

ZARA is about to leave when DEREK enters SL.

DEREK Walter, have you seen Janice?

ZARA *(to WALTER)* Who's this now?

WALTER Oh. That's just... Derek... My neighbour...

ZARA Have you come to get the dog out of the dining room?

DEREK Oh you've met each other? A bit harsh calling her a dog, isn't it?

ZARA What?

WALTER Shut up, Derek! *(to ZARA)* He's a different neighbour. He and Janice live next door.

ZARA I thought Janice was part of the kitchen staff.

DR. GOWER That's right. *(really stretching to make it believable)* They're both the catering staff who also live in the house next door.

ZARA That's handy.

DEREK *(sarcastically)* And very believable.

WALTER Where's Janice?

DEREK I don't know. That's what I came to ask you.

JANICE *(entering from the cupboard, clean now)* I'm here. What's wrong?

WALTER What were you doing in there?

JANICE Oh... I was... err... looking for... spices... for the dinners.

WALTER Why would they be in there? Oh, never mind that. Can you please show Zara out the back door, round the house, back inside and to the toilet please?

JANICE Yes, sir. *(she drags ZARA off in a hurry)*

WALTER *(to DEREK)* You idiot. She thinks there's a dog in there. She wasn't talking about Fran.

DEREK I know that. I've been watching on the cameras, remember.

WALTER Then why did you...

DEREK For fun!

WALTER Arsehole.

FRAN *(hearing his profanity)* Walter!

WALTER *(screams)* Ah! Fran!

FRAN What is taking you so long?

WALTER Sorry. Erm... My neighbour, Derek, here, called over to borrow a cup of milk. I got chatting. Please accept my apologies.

FRAN You've been gone ever so long.

WALTER I'll be through shortly, darling.

JANICE enters SL in a panic.

JANICE *(shouting off SL)* I'll get it for you.

ZARA *(entering SL also)* I can get my own bag.

*Everyone has found themselves standing side by side with **FRAN** on one end and **ZARA** on the other.*

ZARA Could you pass my bag down please?

***WALTER** grabs the bag and passes it **DEREK** who holds it out for **DR. GOWER**. His hands are full, still holding the two meals so takes the handle of the bag with his mouth and passes it on to **JANICE** who passes it over to **ZARA**.*

FRAN *(to ZARA)* Who are you?

*Everyone turns to look at **FRAN** and they all look backwards and forwards at the pair as they each speak over the next few sentences.*

ZARA I'm Zara. Who are you?

FRAN I'm Fran.

ZARA Another one of Walter's neighbours?

FRAN No. I'm on a date.

ZARA Who with?

DEREK *(stepping in to salvage the situation)* With me!

FRAN What?

WALTER What?

JANICE What!

ZARA But I thought you and <u>her</u> *(indicating JANICE)* lived together?

DEREK Oh yeah! Erm... We do! But not like that. We're... *(improvising)* brother and sister!

FRAN *(removing his hand with disgust)* <u>You</u> are <u>not</u> my date! We've only just met! I'm here with...

DR. GOWER *(dumping the two meals into WALTER's arms and linking arms with FRAN)* Allow me to escort you into the dining room. I will send Olivia to fetch you a bottle of wine for your date.

FRAN Oh. Well. I won't say no to that.

DR. GOWER Red, white or rosé?

FRAN Always red! *(they both head into the dining room)*

ZARA What about the dog?

WALTER It's fine. Fran is just in there watching the dog, until the neighbour arrives.

   DR. GOWER returns to the living room.

WALTER OK! Janice! You show Zara to the toilet *(they exit SL)* and doctor, you go tell Olivia what wine Fran wants.

DR. GOWER I don't actually know where she is. I haven't seen her for a while.

WALTER *(shouting off SL)* Olivia!

OLIVIA *(busting out of the cupboard)* Yes Mr. Emerson?

WALTER What the... How many people are in there?

OLIVIA I was just giving my cleaning cupboard the once over. No point cleaning the house with mucky tools.

WALTER Whatever! Could you please grab a bottle of red from the wine cellar please?

OLIVIA *(mumbling as she exits SL)* Always get the shit jobs, I do. Fucking wine cellar... Honestly. I suppose a rack in the kitchen would have been too easy. I shouldn't have to fucking put up with this.

DR. GOWER I'm not quite sure that woman's all there.

WALTER Neither are you, Doctor.

DR. GOWER I beg your pardon!

WALTER I kind of expanded on the whole schizophrenic thing to Fran.

DR. GOWER There was room for expansion?

WALTER I may have told her that sometimes you... you know... pretend to be a dog.

DR. GOWER I have a doctorate. I don't run around the house pretending to be a dog.

WALTER And as my doctor, you need to help me. If you don't back up my story, she's gonna think I'm the one that's mad.

DR. GOWER I think that you're one that's mad.

DEREK Barking mad *(winking at them, proud of his own cheesy pun)*

WALTER Look! The next time I'm alone in here with Fran, just come in and pretend to be a dog, please.

DR. GOWER But look how terrified she is of dogs. This will only make things worse.

DEREK No. That's Zara! Fran is fine with dogs.

DR. GOWER Oh yes. The girl that went to the toilet was Zara wasn't it. Even I'm getting confused now!

WALTER Just wait in the kitchen for when I next get Fran into the living room and do it, please.

DR. GOWER Fine. How will I know when you want me to come in?

WALTER I'll give you a code word. When you hear it, you pounce.

DR. GOWER What will the word be? Barmy?

WALTER That'll do.

DR. GOWER How apt. Would you like me to finish serving dinner first or does acting like a canine take priority?

WALTER *(remembering the dinners)* Of course... The dinners. OK... *(passing the meals on back to him)* Take the dinners back to the kitchen for now, and I'll call for them when I'm ready.

DR. GOWER Very well. *(to himself)* Code word, barmy. Got it. *(exits SL)*

DEREK Quite the pickle you're in.

WALTER I'm well aware, thank you.

OLIVIA enters with a bottle of wine and two glasses, humming joyfully.

WALTER *(to OLIVIA as she passes)* Try and cause as little carnage as possible in there.

OLIVIA You know me, Mr. Emerson. Discretion's my middle name.

WALTER *(aloud as she heads into the dining room)* And try a bit of class if you could.

DR. GOWER *(pokes his head on SL briefly)* Walter! I need your help with the meals. I can't remember which is which.

WALTER Can't anything go right!

WALTER exits SL. OLIVIA arrives in dining room and the lights flip over.

OLIVIA Here you are, missus; a lovely red. None of that cheap shite I drink at home either. *(pours her a glass and places it in front of her at the table)*

FRAN Why don't you join me for a glass? You'd be better company than Walter at the moment.

OLIVIA Go on then. Don't tell Mr. Emerson though. It's an expensive bottle this. I'll just have a smidge. *(takes a big swig from the bottle)*

FRAN Did you end up selling those valuables your friend left to you?

OLIVIA No. I just shoved 'em in a drawer back home. And you'll never guess what. Patricia's popped her clogs as well, now.

FRAN Her friend?

OLIVIA Oh yes! And <u>she's</u> left me a load of junk, too. Fuck knows what I'm going to do with it all. I've just been dumping the lot by my rear door for now. These coffin dodgers are really starting to clutter up my back passage. I moved some of it upstairs, but now my boudoir looks like an episode of Britain's Biggest Hoarders.

FRAN As I've told you before, bring it to me. I'll give it a look over. I wouldn't want you getting swindled on the high street.

OLIVIA I 'spect I might. Would be a nice little earner that would. *(takes another big swig from the bottle, followed by a loud belch)* Well. That's me. Best get back to me cleaning. You enjoy the rest of that. *(indicating the bottle of wine)*

FRAN *(sliding the bottle away from her in disgust)* Please send Walter in if you see him. I'm getting terribly bored.

OLIVIA Righto!

OLIVIA moves into the living room and the lights flip over. She spots DEREK who is still in there.

OLIVIA Cleaning this house is just pointless with you walking around in those scruffy clothes.

DEREK *(sniffing his armpits)* I must admit they are starting to pong a bit. I promise I'll change them the next time I come over.

OLIVIA They must be crawling off ya.

DEREK I just haven't had time to...

OLIVIA Time constraints are no excuse for grubbiness young man. It's no good they're gonna have to come off.

DEREK I'm sorry?

OLIVIA approaches him, grabs his shirt and starts to peel it off.
DEREK wriggles in protest as she tugs at his shirt.

DEREK What are you doing? Stop it!

OLIVIA I'm just gonna stick them in the wash. *(fighting with him)*

DEREK *(trying to break free to no avail)* But I have nothing else to wear.

OLIVIA You've got your birthday suit. *(she manages to relieve him of his top)*

DEREK No! Stop it!

OLIVIA *(trying to get at his bottoms now)* Stop wriggling! *(getting impatient)* Right. I've had enough of this now.

OLIVIA grabs him by the legs and flips him to the floor. DEREK screams.

OLIVIA Just relax whilst I get these off. *(pulls his jeans off)* Just give in to me. It'll be much easier in the long run.

DEREK crawls around the back of the sofa out of the audience's view.
OLIVIA pulls off both his socks on the way there.

OLIVIA You stay put until I get these washed.

OLIVIA sets off towards the dining room, but remembers something.
She turns back towards DEREK.

OLIVIA I forgot your britches! I shall be having those off you as well.

OLIVIA reaches down behind the sofa. Screams from DEREK can be heard as well as a struggle and constant comments from the pair of them. DEREK's bare legs appear in view above the back of the sofa as OLIVIA slides his underwear past his ankles and off.

DEREK *(popping his upper half up from behind the sofa)* OLIVIA! Give me back my clothes.

OLIVIA *(as she heads towards the dining room)* Won't be long.

*The lights come up in the dining room. As **OLIVIA** enters the dining room, her vision obscured by the bundle of clothes, she knocks into **FRAN**'s chair, causing her to spill wine all over her dress.*

OLIVIA Oh bugger!

FRAN Olivia! My dress! It's ruined.

OLIVIA Quick get it off. I'm just about to put a load in. If we wash it now, it'll come out.

FRAN I can't do that. What will I wear?

OLIVIA I'll get you some of my daughter's clothes. She's about your size, you'll be fine. *(**FRAN** is deep in thought)* It'll have to be now, or it won't come out.

FRAN Fine!

* **FRAN** takes her dress off, stripping down to her underwear. She hands it to **OLIVIA**.*

OLIVIA I'll pop it on a hot wash. That'll get the stain out. Probably won't fit when it comes out, but you can't have it all ways, can ya. *(starts to leave)*

FRAN Wait a minute! Where are you going? What about your daughter's clothes?

OLIVIA Oh, they're out in my car.

FRAN What? I thought you meant you had them with you!

OLIVIA I'll get them after I set the washer going. Won't be long. *(exits SR)*

FRAN *(shouting after her)* You can't leave me here like this! What if somebody sees me? *(loud whispering now)* Olivia! Olivia!

* **FRAN** looks around in embarrassment for anything to cover herself up with to no avail. She tiptoes over to the living room. **DEREK** hears her creeping in and quickly disappears behind the sofa. **FRAN** moves in, cautiously, to assure herself that the coast is clear. She spots the large white throw on the back of the sofa and slowly reaches for it. **DEREK**, not wanting her to see him naked, also reaches for the throw. They grab it at the same time. Shocked, upon seeing each other, both tug at the throw from opposite ends and spring back towards each other rolling up inside it.*

FRAN What are you doing?

DEREK I'm trying to conceal my dignity.

FRAN *(tugging at the throw)* Well, find something else.

DEREK *(pulling back)* I was in here first!

FRAN Where are your clothes?

DEREK The cleaner took them!

FRAN She took mine too!

DEREK We need to get them back. Which way did she go?

FRAN That way! *(indicating towards the dining room)*

DEREK We need to co-ordinate our jumps! On three. One. Two. Three!

They carry out a few jumps out this way, making it into the dining room before toppling over onto the floor.

FRAN You idiot!

DEREK Me? You mistimed your jump!

FRAN *(feeling something pressed against her)* Oh my God! Is that your... thing?

DEREK What? *(looking down the throw and realising what she's referencing)* No! I wish! That's my arm.

There's a moment's pause. The pair look at each other, wide-eyed.

DEREK <u>That's</u> my...

FRAN Well can't you control yourself?

DEREK What do you expect with a half-naked woman pressed up against me?

FRAN *(reacts to something)* Hey! Watch where you put that hand.

DEREK It was an accident. I'm a bit restricted.

FRAN Keep your palms closed.

DEREK You're free to leave!

FRAN <u>You</u> leave!

ZARA *(peering in SR)* Hello? *(spotting the pair)* Oh... I thought you two had just met?

FRAN We have!

ZARA *(winking at **DEREK**)* Nice work! Where's the dog gone?

FRAN Could be mowing the lawn or massacring a family of four, depending on what mood he's in.

ZARA What?

DEREK It's gone.

ZARA Thank God for that. I didn't fancy walking all the way back round the outside again. *(she moves to the living room, stepping over the pair awkwardly, and sits on the sofa)*

FRAN OK. We need to stand up! *(they make several failed attempts)* It's no use.

DEREK All this excitement is making me gassy.

FRAN Don't you dare! *(DEREK farts)* You animal! Urgh! That's atrocious

OLIVIA *(entering SR with some clothes)* Here we are. *(sniffing the air)* All right, who's been blasting the arse trumpet.

FRAN Him, of course!

OLIVIA Oh, that's fucking disgusting that is. I'm chewing on it. You wanna airbrush your arse crack after that.

DEREK Better out than in.

OLIVIA Better open a window, more like. *(holding the clothes out to FRAN)* Do you want these then or what?

FRAN Of course. *(stares at DEREK for a moment, waiting for him to act)* Go on then.

DEREK What?

FRAN Leave the blanket so I can get changed.

DEREK No way. I'm <u>completely</u> naked in here. You leave! At least you've got <u>some</u> clothes on!

FRAN Fine! But look away! *(she climbs out of the throw)*

DEREK I think we're <u>way</u> past that!

FRAN In fact. Go in the other room.

DEREK With pleasure. *(exits into the corridor)*

FRAN opens up the clothes she's been given to find that they are not her size and are extremely out of fashion. She stares at the outfit, disgruntled, before putting it on.

OLIVIA What's the matter?

FRAN I doubt this will even fit.

OLIVIA It's a 'one size fits all'.

FRAN I hope no one I know sees me in this.

OLIVIA You cheeky mare! I bought my daughter that from *Bonmarché*! She says it one of her favourites. She's never wore it, mind. Says there's never been an occasion special enough to put it on. You're lucky she keeps accidentally leaving it in my car or you'd have nothing to wear.

FRAN Somehow I doubt it's an accident.

DEREK, still concealed by the throw, enters the living room. He spots ZARA who is facing the SL exit, preventing his escape. He proceeds to

*sneak into the cupboard. Just missing **DEREK**, **DR GOWER** enters SL, gives a courteous nod to **ZARA** and proceeds into the dining room, just after **FRAN** finishes dressing. He places both the meals down.*

DR. GOWER Here is your meal madam. Walter will be joining you shortly. He said not to wait.

FRAN What a surprise. I think I shall just eat this and leave if he doesn't intend to spend any time with me this evening.

DR. GOWER He does apologise. Please blame me for holding him up. *(noticing her clothes)* Did you change?

FRAN Long story.

DR. GOWER Come, Olivia. Don't bother the poor girl!

FRAN *(aside)* It's a little late for that!

*Leaving **FRAN** in the dining room, who takes out her phone to check messages, **DR. GOWER** and **OLIVIA** return to the living room and exit SL, passing **WALTER** who enters with two meals, each on a tray.*

WALTER *(looking at **ZARA**, thinking)* Ah...

ZARA *(pause)* Zara?

WALTER Yes of course. I knew that!

*He joins **ZARA** on the sofa, passing her a tray.*

ZARA *(noticing something)* Walter…

WALTER What?

***ZARA** reaches over to his arm and pulls off the tattoo sleeve, which was slightly creased, giving it away. **WALTER** is at a loss for words..*

WALTER Zara, I…

ZARA Fake tattoo's, fake hair! What's next?

WALTER You know about the wig?

ZARA No more of your lies, Walter. Let's just eat our dinner. *(takes a bite)* Huh…

WALTER What's wrong?

ZARA Oh nothing, nothing. It's just... Is this that fake meat stuff? Like what a vegetarian would eat?

WALTER I thought you <u>were</u> a vegetarian.

ZARA No. I love meat.

WALTER Oh shit! *(sprinting to the other room)*

ZARA *(shouting after him)* What are you doing?

FRAN is just placing a mouthful of meat in her mouth. WALTER rushes over and squeezes her cheeks causing her to spit out the food. He grabs her plate and rushes it back into the other room leaving a gob-smacked FRAN. The lights remain up on both sides. WALTER swaps ZARA's plate with the one in his hand.

WALTER Sorry. This one's yours. This is real meat.
ZARA *(looking at it)* It looks like someone has already chewed some of it.
WALTER That was me. I was testing that it was all right for you.
ZARA And then you spat it back onto my plate?
WALTER Well I didn't want to leave you short.
ZARA *(in disbelief)* Walter. You're bloody barmy!

DR. GOWER is heard barking off SL. ZARA screeches in fear and stands up and starts running around the room scared. Hearing this from the other room, FRAN stands and heads towards the living room.

ZARA It's back. It's back!
FRAN Walter? What's with all the commotion?
WALTER *(shouting to the other room)* Don't come in here.
FRAN I am! I demand to know what is going on.

FRAN enters the corridor between the two rooms. DR. GOWER is still barking. ZARA is still running around screaming.

WALTER Quick! Zara! Hide in the cupboard whilst I get rid of the dog!

WALTER ushers ZARA to the cupboard. He opens the door and shoves her in, but she crashes into DEREK and they both fall out. DEREK is still covering himself with the white throw.

WALTER Where did you come from?
DEREK I was in the closet!
WALTER I knew it! Does Janice know? *(dismissing his own attempt at humour)* No time for jokes. Gimme that!

WALTER, panicking, quickly snatches the white throw from DEREK, leaving him naked again, and throws it over ZARA in an attempt to hide her. DR. GOWER enters at this point running around on all fours pretending to be a dog. At the same time, FRAN enters and sees ZARA under the white throw, wailing and running around the room.

FRAN Ghost! Ghost!

FRAN flees to the dining room, screaming. WALTER chases after her. She exits SR, leaving the house and WALTER standing alone in the dining room.

WALTER Fran, wait, it's…

WALTER sighs and goes into the corridor between rooms. The lights go down in the dining room. ZARA, screaming and running around, crashes into DEREK, who becomes entangled inside the white throw with her. They both fall to the floor, ZARA landing on top of DEREK. She continues to cower in fear. WALTER re-enters the living room and pulls back the throw from ZARA's head. She stops screaming when she realises it isn't a real dog. OLIVIA enters SL.

OLIVIA What's all this fucking racket? Polluting the airways with your incessant drivel!

ZARA *(to DR. GOWER)* What the bloody hell were you doing that for?

DR. GOWER *(pointing at WALTER)* It's him! He ordered me to pretend to be a dog!

WALTER Yes! But not for... Oh never mind.

ZARA Could this date get any more ridiculous? *(she looks down, only just realising that she's on top of DEREK)* What the! *(looks down to his crotch)* Please tell me that's not your…

DEREK Well if you girls are gonna keep throwing yourselves on top of me.

JANICE *(entering SL)* What is goi… *(shouting)* Derek!

DEREK I err… *(gives up)* I'm not even gonna try and explain.

WALTER Right! Enough! Everyone. Clear off so that I can enjoy my date!

DR. GOWER and OLIVIA exit SL followed by DEREK still wrapped in the throw as he chases after JANICE who storms off SL . ZARA turns to WALTER and raids a barrage of slaps on his chest, laughing as she does it.

ZARA You absolute arsehole. I can't believe that you did that to scare me.

WALTER Yeah… ha-ha… I'm a proper joker!

ZARA Oh, Walter. You do know how to have a laugh. I feel so alive when I'm with you.

WALTER That's ironic.

ZARA Even though this is only our second date, there's something about you. I know that you're a bit bizarre, and that half your stories are exaggerated. I'd even go as far as saying that this whole 'bad boy' persona is just a front to try and impress me. I'm not even sure what's going on tonight. All I know is… I like it. I just want to… Want to…

ZARA plants a big kiss on his lips. WALTER enjoys the moment briefly before pushing her off.

WALTER I can't do this.

ZARA What? What's wrong?

WALTER I've not been honest with you. You're a really nice person, Zara. I can't do this to you.

ZARA Do what to me?

WALTER There's something I haven't told you. You should stay well away from me. I can't explain right now. Just know that I'm sorry.

ZARA I don't know what's going on, but I'm going to go. I feel really embarrassed.

WALTER No, please don't. This is my fault.

ZARA If you say so. Just message me when you're ready to explain. See ya, Walter. *(exits SR)*

WALTER lets out a big sigh. Blackout.

Act 2 Scene 2 - Walter Worsens

A few days pass. The lights come up on the living room. DEREK and DR. GOWER are talking. DEREK is finally wearing a change of clothes. JANICE sits on the sofa with the laptop.

DEREK *(spotting JANICE)* What are you doing?

JANICE I'm watching the footage from the other day. Poor Walter.

DR. GOWER Poor Walter? Poor me. I'm the one that was running around the room like a dog.

JANICE Not that. I'm watching after that. He looks so sad. He had his chance with Zara, but he turned her down. I wonder why.

DR. GOWER I think I know why.

DEREK Because he's still in love with Janice?

JANICE Don't be silly, Derek. *(to **DR. GOWER**)* It's not that... is it?

DR. GOWER No, nothing like that. I think it's most likely what I said to him earlier that day.

WALTER *(entering in pyjamas)* Morning! Do you two live here now?

DEREK I'm starting to really like it here, actually.

WALTER *(sarcastically)* Yes, and there's nothing I like more than seeing your face first thing on a morning.

JANICE How's the dating game going?

WALTER OK, I think!

DR. GOWER If the things that happened in this house the other day doesn't turn them off, I don't know what will.

WALTER Well, I've decided to continue with just one girl. It's not fair to either of them to continue seeing both.

JANICE Oooh. Which one?

WALTER I've decided I'm going to only see... *(coughs uncomfortably)*

DR. GOWER Are you OK?

WALTER Yes, just a little cough.

DR. GOWER *(concerned)* Just take it easy, Walter. That's reminds me, I'm going to ring the hospital. Your most recent results should be back by now. *(starts to leave)*

WALTER Doctor, doctor. I've broken my arm in two places.

DR. GOWER Well, I wouldn't visit either of those places again.

WALTER Oh come on. That was my best one.

DEREK Let me try. OK, so a doctor rings up his patient; "I have some bad news and some very bad news," he says. The patient asks for the bad news first. So, the doctor tells him that the lab had called back with his test results, and he only has twenty-four hours to live. The patient responds with, "Twenty-four hours? That's terrible! What's the very bad news?" And the doctor says, "I've been trying to reach you since yesterday."

DR. GOWER *(laughing)* That's very good. I've not heard that one before. *(exits SL)*

DEREK Yes!

WALTER Oh come on!

DEREK Derek, one. Walter, nil!

WALTER That doesn't count. It wasn't even a proper 'Doctor, doctor' joke. *(coughs violently)*

JANICE Walter? Are you OK?

WALTER Yes, I'm... *(coughs)* I'm fine, I just... *(shakes, but remains strong in front of her)* Would you just, *(coughs)* get me some water please, Janice?

JANICE Of course. *(exits SL)*

*When **JANICE** has left the room, **WALTER** collapses on to the floor.*

WALTER *(shaking)* Would you help me please, Derek?
DEREK Erm, yeah. What do you need?
WALTER Just, pull the bed out and help me into it.

***DEREK** runs off SL briefly and wheels the bed on stage. He helps **WALTER** up and onto it. **WALTER** is really struggling and starts to shiver at this point. **DEREK** gets the bed sheets and considerately covers **WALTER** so that he is warm. As he starts to tuck the sheets behind **WALTER**'s shoulder, he throws his arms around **DEREK**, hugging him tightly. **DEREK** feels awkward and doesn't know what to do. A few tears roll down **WALTER**'s face.*

WALTER Thank you, Derek. Please don't tell the others.
DEREK *(understanding)* It's OK, Walter… I won't.

***WALTER** releases him and falls to sleep. Blackout.*

Act 2 Scene 3 - Bed-bound Walter

*When the lights return in the living room, **JANICE** and **DR. GOWER** are in the room as well. **WALTER** is sleeping and hooked up to some machines.*

DR. GOWER *(checking his pulse)* Hmm. His pulse is a little weak, but he should be OK, for now.
WALTER *(waking up)* Doctor?
DR. GOWER Are you feeling OK, Walter?
WALTER I think so. Sorry everyone. Just having a little nap. I'm completely fine!
JANICE No you're not, Walter.
WALTER I'm fine. Stop wittering.
DR. GOWER I'd still like to run some tests. Just to be sure.
WALTER I'm telling you, I'm fine. Look, I'm my usual self; Doctor, doctor. I've broken my arm in two places.

***DR. GOWER** looks at the others, worried.*

WALTER What's wrong?

DR. GOWER No… nothing. I just… I haven't heard that one before, is all. I'm speechless.

WALTER Really?

DR. GOWER Yes, how does it end?

WALTER You're supposed to say 'Well, I wouldn't visit either of those places again'.

DR. GOWER Well, I'll be. A new one for the collection.

WALTER *(really happy)* Yes. I win. *(dozing off again)* I win… I wi…*(falls asleep)*

> *DR. GOWER* and *DEREK* look really worried. *JANICE* begins to cry. Blackout.

Act 2 Scene 4 - Fran's Third Date

A few days pass. Lights return in the living room. The bed is gone.
DEREK is on the sofa with JANICE. DR. GOWER is playing with the laptop.

DR. GOWER You know. I was only joking before, but there's a lot great footage on here. Once Walter, well, you know… We could make a video celebrating his life. This last week or so being the highlights. We could give the money we raise to charity.

JANICE That's a brilliant idea, Doctor Gower.

DEREK I know I'd buy a copy.

JANICE How is Walter, doctor?

DR. GOWER He's the worst I've seen him. His memory dips in and out, which is heart-breaking, because he deals with everything else so well. That's the one thing he hates the most. And he knows when he's going wrong too, which is even more upsetting.

WALTER *(entering, dressed smart-casual)* But I'm not defeated yet.

JANICE *(full of glee)* Walter!

WALTER Here again, I see.

JANICE Sorry we haven't been for a few days. We wanted to give you some rest.

WALTER I appreciate that, but there's nothing to worry about.

JANICE You look different. Are you going somewhere?

WALTER No, I'm having a date over.

JANICE One of the girls?

WALTER Yes.

DEREK Just one?

WALTER Yes, just one.

JANICE Which one?

WALTER That would be telling. *(winks)*

DR. GOWER And no funny outfits today?

WALTER That's right. I thought it best that she meet plain old Walter.

JANICE That's a very good idea. I hope she's worthy of your money.

WALTER We shall see. Now I am going to kindly ask you all to leave.

JANICE What?

WALTER No nonsense. No jokes. No fun and games. Tonight, I wish to be alone. And she'll be here very soon, so if you wouldn't mind.

DR. GOWER Even me?

WALTER Even you, Doctor.

DR. GOWER But it isn't safe for you to be alone.

WALTER I'll be fine for one night.

DR. GOWER Very well. I shall give you <u>most</u> of the evening, but I will return in a few hours to check on you.

WALTER You are too kind. Now, if you'll all excuse me. *(gestures for them to leave)*

JANICE Good luck, Walter.

DR. GOWER, JANICE and DEREK all exit SR. WALTER takes a pen and a piece of paper from his pocket and writes his will. Once finished, he seals it up in an envelope and tucks it behind the urn. The door-bell rings and the lights come up in the dining room. He takes a few deep breaths and then heads into dining room and off SR.

WALTER *(off SR)* Good evening, Fran.

FRAN *(off SR)* Good evening, Walter.

They both enter SR.

WALTER I must say that I am surprised you agreed to come back after last time.

FRAN Well I can't say that I'm overly excited by the idea. But I suppose that some things are worth fighting for.

WALTER That something would be <u>me</u>, I assume?

FRAN Of course it is, silly.

WALTER Good. Let's go and sit in the living room. *(escorting her to the living room)*

FRAN Where is the good doctor tonight?

WALTER We are all alone tonight. I gave him the night off.

FRAN *(with a grin)* So we have the whole house all to ourselves?

WALTER That's right.

FRAN How lovely. Just you, me and the ghost then.

WALTER I'll be honest. That wasn't a ghost.

FRAN It wasn't?

WALTER No, it was a ghoul. Graham the ghoul to be precise. One of the doctor's other personalities. He just threw a sheet over his head to scare you.

FRAN That can't be right. I was sure that was him pretending to be a dog.

WALTER Oh... erm... Of course. No, that was his twin, Antwon!

FRAN His twin?

WALTER Yes. Remember, I told you he had a twin.

FRAN No.

WALTER *(puts his face in his palm)* Of course, that was Zara.

FRAN Are you OK? Maybe you <u>should</u> have your doctor here.

WALTER I'll be fine.

FRAN Well, without your trusted aide, would you like me to make you a drink?

WALTER No, thank you. I don't drink a lot.

FRAN But I make the best tea around. I'd love for you to try it.

WALTER I'm OK, thank you.

FRAN How about a hot chocolate then? Or a glass of water?

WALTER Honestly, I'm fine. I'd like to get cosy in front of the TV if you don't mind.

FRAN Erm... yes. Certainly. *(they both sit on the sofa)* Is everything all right? You seem different tonight.

WALTER Yes, I'm fine. Just a tad tired I suppose.

FRAN Why don't you have a little nap? I wouldn't mind.

WALTER Don't be silly. I couldn't sleep whilst you were here. I wouldn't be able to relax properly.

FRAN Here, let me help you with that. *(starts to give him a shoulder rub)* How does that feel?

WALTER That feels amazing. You've loosened up a bit.

FRAN Well, this is our third date. I don't feel I need to be quite so shy anymore. I feel really comfortable around you, Walter.

WALTER And I, you, Fran.

FRAN's phone goes off and she stops her massage to check her message before resuming the shoulder rub.

WALTER Everything all right?

FRAN Yes, just friends asking for details again. They seem to think that there is this 'rule' where something should happen on the third date.

WALTER *(grinning)* I like the sound of that rule.

FRAN Forget the tea, why don't I go and pour us a glass of wine?

WALTER I'm really not that thirsty.

FRAN Oh go on. Just a little tipple.

WALTER You're really obsessed with making me a drink, aren't you?

FRAN I just want to show you how good to you I can be.

WALTER *(referring to his shoulder rub)* You already are.

FRAN How about a snack then?

WALTER But I've already eaten tonight. *(cheekily)* Maybe if I was to… work up an appetite.

FRAN I think we can manage that.

FRAN pushes him onto his back and pulls the throw over both of them. Blackout. When the lights return they are both laid on the sofa, smiling.

WALTER That, was, amazing.

FRAN It really was.

WALTER Now I <u>am</u> thirsty.

FRAN I'll go and pour us a glass of water.

FRAN climbs off the sofa, collects her stray garments and re-dresses herself. She exits SL. WALTER also re-dresses himself. He stands and stretches his whole body out with a huge smile on his face. FRAN returns with two glasses of water. She hands one to WALTER before drinking hers.

FRAN Phew! I really needed that. I'd better just quickly check in with my friends.

FRAN heads over to her phone to check her messages. As she does this WALTER pours his glass of water into the nearby plant pot. He wipes his lips as she turns around.

WALTER Thanks, Fran. I was parched

FRAN Don't mention it.

WALTER I think you must worn me out. I'm feeling really sleepy all of a sudden. *(he sits on the sofa)* I think I just need a quick nap. Why don't you join me?

FRAN With pleasure!

*She joins **WALTER** on the sofa. She cuddles up to him and they lay down. She starts stroking his face.*

WALTER That feels great. Really relaxing.
FRAN You just drop off.

*__WALTER__'s eyes begin to close and they both fall to sleep. After a few moments **FRAN** 'wakes' up and slowly climbs off the sofa so as not to disturb **WALTER** who is snoring loudly. **FRAN** goes back to her phone and makes a phone call. She walks into the dining room whilst it is ringing. Her posh voice is gone when the recipient of the call answers..*

FRAN Hello? Yeah, he's lights out. Are you still parked around the corner? Good! Hurry up. I'll let you in.

*A few moments later, an old van can be heard pulling up to the house. **FRAN** exits SR and returns, followed by a rough looking man. **FRAN** points to the vases, the coin collection, the weapons and the painting. The man takes them off SR in a few trips. Once the house has been cleared out, she ushers him off SR. She has one last look around and then heads back into the living room and carefully slides herself back onto the sofa besides **WALTER**. Blackout. The lights return and the scene is exactly as it was. **WALTER** wakes and he also 'wakes' **FRAN** up, at the same time.*

WALTER Morning beautiful.
FRAN *(back to posh)* Morning? *(checks her watch)* We've only been asleep an hour, silly.
WALTER It feels like much longer.
FRAN It is quite late. I suppose I really should be going. *(climbing off the sofa)*
WALTER That's a shame.
FRAN I know, but I must. I have an early start in the morning.
WALTER *(climbing off the sofa also)* I'll come and see you out.
FRAN I should expect you would.

*They both head into the dining room. **WALTER** spots the empty shelves and missing items. **FRAN** 'notices' too and 'reacts.'*

FRAN Oh my word. What's happened?

WALTER Well unless Doctor Gower has developed a Richard the robber personality, I'd say I've been robbed.

FRAN Oh, Walter. I'm so sorry.

WALTER I can't believe this.

FRAN Someone must have broken in whilst we were sleeping.

WALTER Yeah. Either that or, you slipped me a sleeping drug, waited for me to fall asleep, let your friend into the house, had him steal everything of value and then came back to bed so that I'd been none the wiser of your involvement.

FRAN *(stuttering)* What? I've never been so insulted in all my life. What gives you an absurd idea like that?

WALTER The night of our first date, when you excused yourself to go to the toilet, I took a sneaky peek at your phone. I only wanted to see what you were saying to your friends about me. Naturally I was a little amused when instead I saw how you were planning to con me.

FRAN *(posh voice is dropped)* You went through my phone? How dare you?

WALTER Oh, God forbid! Did I do something immoral? Why don't we talk about something illegal? Like theft!

FRAN You've known all along. All this time? Why didn't you stop me?

WALTER I still wanted to get you into bed. You're still attractive... On the outside.

FRAN Well then. We're both winners. You got what you wanted. And I got what I wanted. Those valuables will bring in a pretty penny when we sell them.

WALTER Actually <u>you</u> didn't get what <u>you</u> wanted. Knowing <u>exactly</u> what you intended to steal, I knew <u>exactly</u> what to replace with cheap knock-offs.

FRAN *(annoyed)* What!

WALTER That's right! The coins, the vases, the weapons. The money painting.

FRAN *(snapping)* It's Monet!

WALTER *(snapping back)* Whatever! I'd say everything you stole is worth about, a hundred quid. If you're lucky. Oh and, by the way. I never drank the drugged water. It was quite amusing pretending to be asleep whilst you carried out your pointless scheme. The plant in the living room on the other hand may be a little drowsy.

FRAN You son of a...

WALTER Oh, and this room has CCTV, so the police will no doubt wish to speak to you when I show them the evidence of you stealing from me.

FRAN *(looking for the camera, nervously)* I can't believe you played me like this.

WALTER Sorry. *(shrugs)*

FRAN Why not just have me arrested and sleep with someone else?

WALTER Well, you see. That's the other thing. I couldn't sleep with <u>any</u> girl, or believe me, it wouldn't have been you.

FRAN What do you mean?

WALTER I have my own reasons for not wanting to get too close to anyone right now. My good doctor made me see that. I wasn't about to give up on my quest for pleasure, but I'm also not a bad man. I wouldn't dream of leading someone on who I <u>actually</u> liked.

FRAN So you just used me?

WALTER *(a big grin appears)* Don't play the victim with me. What do you do? Meet people online, scope out the valuables, and then have your friend rob them?

FRAN It's kind of my thing.

WALTER Well, it's over now. Why don't you grab a chair and I'll give the police a call?

FRAN makes a run for the exit towards SR. WALTER grabs her by the wrist. She swings her other hand around and punches him square in the chest causing him to clutch it, releasing her. WALTER struggles on his feet. FRAN stares at him, realising she's caused some serious harm. WALTER tries to keep his composure so as not to appear weak in front of FRAN.

WALTER *(quietly and angrily)* Get out! *(she doesn't move)* GET OUT!

FRAN scurries off SR. WALTER stumbles over landing face down. Blackout. The lights come up on the dining room only to the exact same scene. DR. GOWER enters SR. He sees WALTER and rushes to his side.

DR. GOWER *(panicking)* Walter!

Blackout.

Act 2 Scene 5 - Ending

The lights come up in the living room where DR. GOWER, JANICE and DEREK are crowded around WALTER who is laying on his bed in

*the living room. He is hooked up to the drip and the E.C.G. machine
which is beeping normally.*

JANICE Is he going to be OK?

DR. GOWER I'm afraid not. He has so many things wrong with him and
they're all getting rapidly worse.

WALTER *(weakly)* I'm OK. Stop worrying about me.

DR. GOWER You're not OK, Walter. This is serious. What happened?

DEREK Did you get frisky with Fran?

DR. GOWER Frisky?

WALTER *(still weak)* You know... *(lifting hips off of bed)* frisky! And,
yes I did.

DEREK Congratulations. You did it.

DR. GOWER But what about what I told you? I'd hoped you wouldn't
go through with it.

WALTER Don't worry, Doctor. Turns out she was just a common thief.
I've known all along, but decided it best not to tell you lot. I didn't
want you to worry. I got what I set out for. And she got what she
deserved.

DR. GOWER I see.

JANICE I don't. Tell me.

WALTER You'll have to watch the footage on the laptop later. *(coughs
heavily)* I don't think I have the energy to tell you the whole story.
(DR. GOWER) You'll find your painting in the spare room upstairs,
along with everything else from the dining room. *(coughs violently)* I
think this is it, Doctor. I can feel it.

DR. GOWER Save your strength, Walter.

WALTER I know, but I want one last shot at it.

DR. GOWER Shot at what?

WALTER Doctor, doctor. You have to help me out.

DR. GOWER Oh dear. Fine, go on.

WALTER That's it.

DR. GOWER That's what?

WALTER That's the whole of the patient's line.

DR. GOWER It can't be. I don't know any that begin like that.

WALTER Don't be playing with me, again, Doctor. I know I'd
accidentally said that joke twice the other day. You're not pretending
you haven't heard it to be nice again, are you?

DR. GOWER No, really. I haven't heard this one. How does it end?

WALTER *(joking)* Oh no, I can't. I can see the light. I'm going towards
it.

DR. GOWER *(chuckling)* Stop messing around and tell me.

WALTER No can do, Doc. I'll take it the grave with me. *(coughs loudly)*

DR. GOWER Are you OK?

WALTER I will be.

JANICE *(crying)* I don't want you to go.

DEREK Neither do I. I instinctively didn't like you for obvious reasons. But... I was wrong. I've had loads of fun these past couple of weeks. I'll actually miss you.

WALTER I still hate you.

JANICE Walter!

WALTER I'm kidding. Maybe in another life, Derek. We could have been good friends.

ZARA *(enters from the dining room)* Walter?

WALTER Zara?

ZARA What's happening?

WALTER What are you doing here?

ZARA Your cleaner let me in. You never rang me, and I needed to know what was going on. I'm sorry, I should have messaged you before just turning up like this.

WALTER It's OK. It's good to see you.

ZARA What's wrong with you?

WALTER That little illness I told you about... Well it's not so little.

ZARA Are you... dying?

WALTER Afraid so.

ZARA But... But...? I'm so sorry, Walter. When you didn't message me, I thought you weren't interested. I've called you every name under the sun to my friends.

WALTER Don't worry about it. You weren't to know. I only wish I had the time to get to know you better.

ZARA Walter.

WALTER I've made so many <u>real</u> friends in the end. In answer to your question, Doctor; It's yes.

DR. GOWER What question?

WALTER I would have given up all the money in the world, just to spend a little more time with you fine people.

JANICE Oh, Walter.

WALTER Janice. You know me so well. You knew, just from talking to me on the phone, that something was wrong. I'm sorry that I never realised, that I had the best thing that had ever happened to me, all along. I'm so glad, that I got to spend time with you again, before it was too late. You helped me have the best weeks of my life and that's something that all the money in the world can't buy. *(looks at*

DEREK) Derek. I'm glad that I got to know you. I feel so guilty over the way that I treated Janice when we were young, that I thought I could never forgive myself. But the universe works itself out, as it always does. I'm so glad, that she has you to take care of her. *(looks at ZARA)* Zara. Seeing how upset you are at this situation has made me realise how stupid my little game was. I was wrong to involve anyone new in my life, knowing I would be dead soon. You don't deserve this upset and grief. But I am so glad that I met you. Please don't give up on relationships. You are a wonderful human being. Thank you for being a part of my life in the end. *(looks at DR. GOWER)* Alan. Can I call you Alan? It doesn't seem right calling you Doctor Gower now. You are so much more than an employee to me. I can tell that you genuinely care about my health, and not the money. I hope I didn't push you too far. You were the best friend that I've ever had. *(looks around at them all)* I love you all, so much. *(they all share a tearful smile)* Now I feel that... *(coughs very violently)* I'm just going to have a little nap. *(his eyelids are heavy)* A little sleep... *(dozes off)*

JANICE Walter?

DR. GOWER Let him sleep. He's right, you know. You only truly understand yourself in the end, and what you really wanted all along. Money bought him happiness for all these years, but in the end, he wanted something different. We all need to remember that.

DEREK He really is a remarkable person.

ZARA I feel so helpless.

DR. GOWER It's OK, Zara. There's nothing any of us can do. I'm sure that you being here is helping him tremendously.

The E.C.G. machine flat-lines. JANICE begins crying. DEREK comforts her. ZARA is very tearful. DR. GOWER covers WALTER with the sheet. They all mourn WALTER's passing for a few moments. After some time, DR. GOWER unplugs the machine to silence it.

ZARA I can't believe I barely knew him, and it's still so sad.

DEREK And you will most likely be rich now.

ZARA What do you mean?

JANICE The whole reason he went on the internet, was to find someone he could leave all of his money to. My guess is, that you are the winner.

ZARA I don't feel like a winner.

DR. GOWER You know, I have no idea where he would have left his will.

*An envelope from behind the clock falls onto the floor. Everyone notices this. **DR. GOWER** picks it up an opens it.*

JANICE What is it, Doctor?
DR. GOWER It's… Walter's will.

*They all stare at **WALTER**'s body, feeling spooked. The four of them share glances with each other for a few moments.*

DEREK What does it say?
DR. GOWER It says how his money is to be divided. It says… *(wells up a little)* That…I… *(takes a moment)* get half of everything he owns. *(he takes another moment to take it it)* The rest is to be divided between you three and the cleaner.
JANICE Really?
ZARA Really?
DEREK *(giddy)* Yes!

*The others stare at **DEREK** for his insensitivity.*

DEREK *(noticing the others and composing himself)* I mean… Aw! That was nice of him…
DR. GOWER The five of us have just become very rich people.
JANICE I can't believe it.
ZARA I know. I don't know if I feel comfortable taking all that money from him. This is only the third time I've met him.
JANICE I feel the same. I've only recently come back into his life. It seems wrong that I should benefit from that.

***ZARA** and **JANICE** turn to look at **DEREK**. He does a double take when he notices them staring.*

DEREK What? I have absolutely no problem taking the money.
JANICE *(sincerely)* I just don't know if we can accept it.
DEREK *(putting his hands forcefully on her shoulders)* But we will.
DR. GOWER *(triumphantly)* Well which way did you come in!
JANICE, DEREK & ZARA What?
DR. GOWER "Well which way did you come in" is the answer.
DEREK What are you talking about?

DR. GOWER Walter said, "Doctor, doctor. You have to help me out." And I say, "Of course. Which way did you come in?" It's so simple. How did I not get it?

DEREK Because it was… Meant to be.

JANICE I think it's time we all left. Let's give Walter some peace.

DR. GOWER I have a very special bottle in the dining room. I think now would be an appropriate time to open it.

*Lights come up in the dining room and they all head in there. **DR. GOWER** grabs a bottle and glasses from just off SR and pours everyone a glass. Meanwhile, **OLIVIA** enters SL. She is cleaning when she notices someone under the sheet. She lifts it up.*

OLIVIA What you doing under there, Walter? Playing sardines? Well I need to give the bed the once over. Don't worry, I'll work around you.

She rolls him onto his side to clean under him, but as she tugs on the sheet he rolls out of bed onto the floor. The noise alerts the others.

OLIVIA Oops! Sorry, Walter. Let's get you on the sofa. *(tries to lift him)* Jesus, you're a dead weight.

The others rush into the living room.

DR. GOWER *(shouting)* Olivia! What are you doing?

OLIVIA I'm moving Walter. He's making the place look untidy. It's unsightly.

JANICE Olivia! Have some respect for the dead.

OLIVIA Dead? Who's dead?

DR. GOWER Walter!

OLIVIA Oh fuck me! *(drops him)* Not another one! I'll be unemployed at this rate. Between him and those old bats up at Midgely Retirement Home, the undertaker round here's gonna be busy! He'll be knocking up wooden overcoats at the rate of knots. Well, we can't just leave him on the floor. I heard people shit their britches when they die. I don't wanna be getting the rug doctor out again.

*They all help **WALTER** back into bed.*

DR. GOWER Come on, Olivia. Why don't you join us for a glass in the dining room?

OLIVIA Don't mind if I do. I'm fucking knackered. Lifting a cadaver is thirsty work.

They all move back to the dining room. **DR. GOWER** *pours another drink and hands it to* **OLIVIA.**

DR. GOWER To Walter!
ALL To Walter!

They all take a sip. **DEREK** *and* **JANICE** *share a loving kiss.*

ZARA Oh my God. *(puts her hand over her mouth)* I think I'm gonna be sick.
JANICE What's wrong?
ZARA You two. Brother and sister! Kissing!

All except **ZARA** *and* **OLIVIA** *have a good chuckle.*

DEREK We aren't really brother and sister.
ZARA What?
JANICE Long story! We'll explain later.

They all continue to drink for a few moments as they reflect on recent events.

DR. GOWER I'm going to miss him challenging me with his jokes.
JANICE Can I try? Doctor, doctor. What happened to the man who fell into a circular saw and had the whole left side of his body cut away?
DR. GOWER He's all right now.

All the lights slowly fade out, except a single spotlight on **WALTER**'s *corpse which lingers for a few moments longer, before slowly fading out also.*

End of Act II

Walter Ego was first performed on April 6th 2022 at the Academy Theatre in Barnsley by Wakefield Little Theatre with the following cast and production team;

Walter	Fraser Sugden
Dr. Gower	Andrew Parkin
Janice	Joanna Goldson
Derek	Andrew Crossland
Fran	Faye Benning
Zara	Nicky Rainford
Olivia	Zoe Parkin

Directed by	Andrew Crossland

Producer	Helen Grace
Stage Manager	Rebecca Firth
Costumes	Elizabeth Hampton & Betty Marsden
Stage Designer	Mathilde Lemelsle
Light & Sound	Debby Pickering & Susie Rowley
Props	Pauline Taylor
Prompt	Sheila Priest
Poster Design	Debby Pickering
Programme	Susie Rowley

Set suggestion:-

Credit:- Mathilde Lemelsle

Special Thanks To:-

Wakefield Little Theatre Committee – For allowing me to stage my script and funding its production.
Christine Mulrooney – For editing versions of the script.
Julie Holland – For whom hugely inspired the character Olivia.
For attending script readings and providing feedback – Dean Love, Alice Willerton, Ashley Ironmonger, Bob Willerton, Michael Cutts, Sophie Goddard, Esther Dyson, Jo Upson, Richard Caile, Hugh Jones, Jane Laverack, Helen Watson, Keith Watson, Gail Rogers, Helen Grace, Faye Benning, Paul Haley, Joanna Goldson, Debby Pickering.
For taking the time to read the script alone and provide feedback – Eloise Garbutt.
Minor script contributions – Phillip Sharpe, James Grainger.

Thank you to all who were involved in any way. Big or small.

Andrew Crossland

Printed in Great Britain
by Amazon